ink and ashes

Young Adult Romance

The Haunted Hearts Series
Book Two

lia lucas

Ink and Ashes
The Haunted Heart Series - Book 2
Copyright © 2024 by Lia Lucas
All rights reserved.

Book Cover and formatting provided by Trisha Fuentes
https://bit.ly/m/trishafuentes

No part of this book may be reproduced in any form or by any electronic or mechanical means, including information storage and retrieval systems, without written permission from the author, except for the use of brief quotations in a book review.

ISBN: 979-8-3303-1599-4 (Paperback)

**Published by
Ardent Artist Books**
www.ardentartistbooks.com

about ardent artist books

➥ ABOUT US

Ardent Artist Books was established in 2008

We publish modern and historical romances once a month!

Get Your FREE List: Published & Upcoming Books
visit our website at:
https://bit.ly/3Wva4o0

* * *

➥ WE HAVE BOOK TRAILERS

Follow us on YouTube!
https://bit.ly/3W3xn7a

Like, Subscribe & Comment

➥ WE HAVE SERIALIZED FICTION!

Visit our website today to download one of our stories that unfold in bite-sized pieces!

Each installment is just 99¢!

https://bit.ly/3LsDpJL

* * *

➥ LET'S CONNECT!

Fuel your love of fiction with exclusive content and captivating insights from Ardent Artist Books. Whether you crave the thrill of modern narratives or the timeless elegance of historical fiction, our newsletter delivers a curated selection straight to your inbox. Plus, as a welcome gift, receive a FREE downloadable eBook:

"The Family Fix"
https://bit.ly/49BR3UB

1
the letter of inheritance

*A*nya Petrov perched at her desk, a haven buried in a mountain of books, knickknacks, and crumpled paper. Sunlight streamed through her window, casting dappled patterns on the worn wooden floor. The golden beams ignited the motes of dust dancing in the air, each glimmer reminiscent of the dreams she chased like fireflies. Anya's long, wavy blonde hair cascaded down her shoulders, reflecting the light in strands that matched the faded colors of antique pages. Anya's green eyes scanned the cluttered journal entries. She thought deeply, lost in her imagination.

Anya sighed and turned back to her writing. The pages held her unfinished story, a tale that captivated her but was held back by her self-doubt. Characters hovered at the edges of her mind, their words trapped behind the fog that obscured her creativity. Anya's fingers tapped an impatient beat on the desk, a persistent reminder of her desire to revive the story, even if the ink barely spoke.

Anya slumped in her chair, the summer heat wrapping around her like an oppressive blanket. She absently flipped through her notebook, an entangled mess of half-formed ideas and abandoned characters strewn across the pages like lost souls. The vibrant colors of the season outside contrasted sharply with her dull surroundings. Kids from her neighborhood laughed and chased one another; their voices, full of life, floated through her window and mingled with the salty scent of the ocean breeze. Once, the thought of writing made her feel free—like a kite soaring high on the wind. Now, the very idea of picking up her pen felt as laborious as moving an entire house. Anya yearned to write, to pour her thoughts into the blank pages, but the words felt heavy, as if bound by invisible chains that threatened to drag her under.

The impending deadline hung over her like a guillotine, demanding the creation of something extraordinary to pass her creative writing class. Anya had always dreamed of being a writer, but now, the pressure felt stifling—each unwritten story mocked her from the confines of her mind. She glanced at the old typewriter propped against the wall, a relic from the past, and wondered if it would come to life under her fingertips. But even imagining its clatter sent shivers of doubt through her. Moments flickered in her memory—nights spent scribbling under the pale glow of a lamp, fueled by caffeine and careless passion. The fire that once ignited her imagination now simmered, a stubborn ember resisting the kindling of creativity.

She noticed a large, out-of-place envelope among the mess on her desk. *How did this get here?* She felt curious but also nervous as she reached for it hesitantly. Holding the envelope made her feel uneasy, as if it connected her to a distant past. She wondered what secrets it contained and why it made her palms sweat against its crisp surface.

Her heart thudded against her ribcage as she pried it open, the old-fashioned paper crackling like the brittle leaves outside in autumn. As the contents spilled onto her desk, a faint scent leached out, carrying with it the musk of aged parchment. It clashed with the sweetness of her lavender air freshener, an odd mixture that sent her mind wandering to dusty attics and forgotten treasures. She unfolded the letter with care, each movement imbued with a sense of gravity that seemed to hang in the air.

"Dear Anya," it began, the handwriting ornate and looping like branches entwined with mystery. The words tumbled forward, detailing the inheritance of Dvor House from her great-uncle, a name she barely recalled. Her breath caught in her throat as she pieced together the hushed family conversations, the fleeting mentions of the once-grand estate that now sat at the edge of her small town. A chill swept through her at the unspoken tales of wails echoing through its empty halls and shadows creeping in the windows.

As she read deeper, excitement filled her. This mansion could hold the key to unlocking her past, a treasure trove of stories waiting to be lived and breathed through her writing. But, like the sudden gusts of autumn wind, that exhilaration quickly curled, enveloping her in a thick fog of dread. She skimmed over the lines of the letter again, the words etching themselves into her mind—her unique "gift." A haunting reminder of her ability to see and communicate with spirits, the very essence of who she was, surged within her. It was a legacy she had never asked for, a responsibility that loomed heavy, sending quakes of uncertainty through her core.

Anya felt the weight of the letter in her hands, aware of the excitement it held. It gave her the chance to become the mansion's new caretaker, but that role also raised worries about stepping into a world filled with both brightness and shadows. *Did she really want a life marked by ghostly visits and strange nighttime sounds?* Memories of her childhood came back—stories told around the fire, the nervous glances shared with friends as they dared each other to face their fears of the unknown.

Her thoughts spun, tethering her to the memories until voices from yesteryear coaxed her to revisit the faint ghost tales. "You're bound to the haunted Dvor," they'd whispered, careful not to awaken the spirits they believed lurked there.

That unsettling dread curled again in her chest as she recalled the tales of lost souls—how they wandered the halls, eternally tethered to the past, aching for completion—or revenge. *What if she became ensnared in a story that wasn't hers?*

Anya dropped the letter, trembling slightly, the surface of her desk suddenly feeling like a rickety boat afloat in choppy waters. The older relatives she'd visited at family gatherings always spoke of her abilities with a mix of admiration and concern. They'd dissected her empathy like a mesmerizing puzzle, all the while cautioning her about its burdens. The pressure of expectation bore down on her. Could she confront whatever waited for her at Dvor?

Sitting still, Anya pressed her palm against the smooth surface of her desk. She stared at the letter, an artifact of her journey that had only just begun. The words danced on the page—an invitation and a curse. A bittersweet rush of purpose began to unfurl within her. With a sharp breath, she embraced the swirling myriad of emotions. *Yes, it was terrifying, but if she accepted this legacy, it meant embracing her identity, right?* Perhaps Dvor House held more than things that went bump in the night; it could unveil her connection to the past and even grant her the inspiration to finish her story.

Her heart sped up, mixing excitement and worry. Anya's determination grew, her messy feelings turning into resolve. She looked around her room—the clutter matched her jumbled thoughts, full of promise and doubt. But in that mess was the spark to create, the energy to turn scattered ideas into something special. She'd made a choice. All that was left was to unlock the door to Dvor House and see what lay behind those haunted walls.

Anya picked up the letter again, feeling the weight of history in her hands, her heart racing with unanswered questions. Solitude or a solution? Inspiration or a trap? With nervous anticipation, she set her notebook aside, a new vision igniting in her mind. As possibilities swirled before her, she whispered, "What if?"

And she took a deep breath; her journey had begun.

* * *

ANYA TOOK a deep breath as she looked around her bedroom one last time, surrounded by the scent of fading lavender and old paper. Her eyes moved from the walls covered in posters of her favorite authors to the stack of journals, each filled with dreams, heartbreaks, and the whispers of beings not of this world. She ran her fingers along the edge of one worn journal, its spine cracked like her nerves, and thought of the stories that would go untold without her.

Her heart pounded, and with her palms slick against the coarse fabric of her oversized sweater, she stuffed the journals into her duffel bag alongside carefully curated candles, talismans of protection, and a few well-worn books. A chill raced through the room as if the air itself could sense her apprehension, and shadows seemed to swell, tracing her movements like curious spirits.

"Keep it together," she murmured under her breath, the rational part of her mind seeking to silence the swirling mass of anxiety.

She sensed the weight of the unknown pressing down on her, an oppressive fog wrapping around her heart and squeezing.

"Okay, just a mansion. Just stones and bricks," she told herself, trying to convince her racing heartbeat. But the childhood whispers of ghost stories, those mischievous tales spun by her friends, echoed in her mind. They painted the mansion as a land of lost souls, forever trapped in their agonies.

In the car, as she traveled the winding roads lined with towering trees, Anya shifted in her seat, drumming her fingers nervously against her thigh. Outside, the scenery blurred past—a dull wash of greens and browns giving way to endless reminders of what lay ahead. Each tree, with its gnarled branches reaching out like forlorn fingers, signified a memory she couldn't afford to confront, no matter how much she wished to help those beyond the grave.

Conflicting feelings fought inside her; she wanted to accept her role as a medium, the careful art of hearing the troubled spirits that roamed through time. Yet, the weight of that responsibility pressed on her like a heavy stone. The lives she could influence—what if she couldn't help them? What if she only caused them more pain? Beneath her skin, a pulse of doubt matched the beating in her chest.

"Anya, are you okay?" her mother's voice broke through her tangled thoughts, laced with concern.

"Yeah, just... thinking," Anya stammered, forcing a weak smile. The conversation shifted to trivial matters, and she let herself sink back into silence, grateful for the distraction yet keenly aware of the tension stretching between her and her mother.

When they arrived, the mansion loomed ahead, a magnificent yet terrifying sight. She stepped from the car, her breath hitching in her throat. Dvor House, with its crumbling stones covered in thick ivy, seemed to breathe with life, holding a history she could barely begin to fathom. The tall, arched windows glimmered under the changing light, resembling watchful eyes of deceased souls waiting for her to ascend the hallowed steps.

A breeze tugged at her unruly hair, sending shivers racing across her arms, and she hesitated at the entrance. The grand wooden door stood heavy, rustic and aged, its surface telling stories etched in time. Part of her felt anchored to the ground, paralyzed by the weight of doubt. *What awaited her inside? What spirits would she meet? Would they share their joy or their sorrow?*

Anya's mother stepped out of the car, her heels clicking against the cobblestone driveway. She smoothed down her blouse, stealing glances at Dvor House and the mysteries it bore. With a forced smile, she turned to Anya, her voice warm but tinged with caution. "I'll be across the street, talking to the neighbors about the history of this place. They've been here for years and might have some interesting stories. I need you to wait for me before you walk inside, okay?"

Anya nodded, an absent gesture that barely registered as her eyes roamed around the enormous fading structure. The intricate carvings on the door caught her attention, drawing her in like a moth to flame. Words from her mother faded into the background, a dull drone eclipsed by the mansion's allure and her burning curiosity. Maybe it was impulsive, maybe reckless, but the call of the house was too great to resist. With a quick glance at her mother, who turned away to focus on the neighbors, Anya pushed the heavy door open. It creaked ominously, like a long-held secret exhaling its first breath after years of silence. The cool air rushed to greet her, wrapping around her like an embrace, both inviting and unnerving, as she stepped inside on her own.

The foyer welcomed her with an air of nostalgia, the smell of dust and worn wood creating an atmosphere rich with both sorrow and beauty. Sunlight poured through the tall, arched windows, casting ethereal beams that almost danced in the shadows surrounding her. Anya stepped forward, the floorboards groaning underfoot, as her heart raced with exhilarating fear. There was something electric in the air, a sense of waiting that thrummed beneath her skin. Each step she took pulled her deeper into the mansion, deeper into its stories, and as she wandered through the expansive room, a tingle of anticipation mingled with an underlying trepidation. What lay ahead, she couldn't yet grasp, but she felt an urgency that told her she needed to uncover whatever secrets whispered through the halls of Dvor House.

The walls, adorned with remnants of art long forgotten, seemed to beckon her forward. Anya glanced up at the magnificent chandelier that hung precariously above her, crystals glinting like trapped stars. A shiver danced down her spine, and she paused under its luminous gaze, feeling the weight of countless pairs of eyes that had once gathered here in laughter and celebration. The thought sent a rush of warmth over her, yet an unsettling chill still flickered in the corners of her mind. "You're here now," she whispered to herself, trying to channel the confident persona she had always envisioned. "You can do this."

As she crossed the threshold into another room, Anya's breath caught. The parlor opened up before her, a mismatched collection of furniture sprawled across the space with an air of untamed elegance. An intricately carved rocking chair creaked softly, as if a gentle breeze propelled it in rhythm with memories lost. Anya walked deeper into the room, her fingers brushing against the frayed upholstery of an old couch, feeling the history seep into her skin. Outside, the laughter of her mother and the neighbors bounced along the cobblestones like a foreign echo, but inside, all that existed was a profound stillness.

Anya felt the pull of her own thoughts, wrestling with her desire to be a part of this forgotten world. "What stories have you kept hidden?" she murmured, half-expecting an answer from the shadows themselves. Almost immediately, a sharp chill rushed past her, a whisper of something unspoken that sent goosebumps skittering across her arms. She closed her eyes for a moment, trying to capture the sensation, the feeling of something watching her, something wanting to communicate. Her heart thudded louder in her chest as she opened her eyes, feeling the electricity in the air growing thicker, drawing her closer to whatever secrets lay in wait.

She began to wander again, arching her neck to absorb the faded wallpaper, and glimpses of brighter days faded beneath layers of time. Each room held a haunting elegance, remnants of past lives nestled within tattered corners and aged mahogany furniture. Unfinished stories lingered, coated in dust and regrets, swirling in the air as if begging to be released. Anya felt more alive in this moment than she had in months, wrapped in the enchanting mystery that the dying mansion promised. A connection formed with every inch she explored, as if she were beginning to unlock the house's heart.

But that pulse, so intoxicating, was threaded with unease. She recoiled slightly at the realization that she had come alone. The room danced with shadows, and Anya couldn't shake the sensation that perhaps she had stumbled too far into something that was beyond her grasp. Yet, whatever fear lingered in her stomach was overshadowed by an insatiable curiosity. *What awaited her within these walls?* The question resonated between her ears, pushing her feet forward, further into the depths of the mansion.

Outside, her mother gestured animatedly to the neighbors, discussing the house and its history, but Anya lost herself in the siren call of the interior, fixated on the potent mix of emotions that entwined like grave vines around her heart. Resolved, she edged toward another doorway at the end of the parlor, the promise of discovery flickering just beyond. She clenched her fists, willing herself to embrace whatever came next, determined to unlock the secrets that awaited her inside Dvor House.

"If only you could talk," she muttered softly, and her own voice echoed, mingling with the phantom sounds that danced around her. The remnants of laughter, stories of love and loss resided here, embedded in every crevice and shadow. She felt a strange pull, an almost magnetic force urging her to delve deeper, to listen beyond the surface.

But doubts flickered in her mind like candle flames wavering in a storm.

What if she couldn't handle their grief? What if their sorrow crushed her spirit like a heavyweight?

An underlying current of fear held her firmly in place, yet the unmistakable desire to explore flooded her veins. She refused to let those doubts tether her down.

"Just another day, Anya," she breathed, clenching her hands into fists.

2
arrival

The air shifted, and she felt it cling to her skin. The musty scent of age enveloped her like a shroud—a fusion of dust, forgotten memories, and the faintest hint of something floral long since wilted.

In the foyer, she saw a sweeping staircase curl gracefully toward the upper levels, its banister intricately carved with swirling designs that hinted at the artistry of its creators. A large chandelier draped from the high ceiling, its crystals casting prismatic rainbows onto the walls. Many pieces had fallen, littering the floor like fallen stars, contributing to the air of elegant decay that permeated the air.

Anya paused, her breath hitching as the realization sank in—the mansion was alive, each creak and whisper softening her apprehensions. It felt like stepping into a story that had been waiting just for her. A shiver rippled down her spine, excitement rivaling fear. Her intuition didn't steer her wrong; she had a bond with this place, a connection that pulsed beneath her skin.

A soft sound broke the silence—a barely audible sigh, as if the house breathed along with her. She turned slightly, her wide green eyes scanning the empty space. *Had she heard that?*

"Hello?" Her voice sounded thin against the vastness of the foyer, swallowed almost instantly by the shadows.

No response came, just the creaking of old wood and the flutter of—what was that? Her heart raced again as she spotted movement in the periphery.

A fluttering figure caught her eye: a piece of fabric, perhaps, shifted in the dim light. Anya approached carefully, stepping lightly to avoid disturbing the dust that swirled around her. The tension in the air climbed higher with each heartbeat, anticipation tingling in her fingertips.

As she neared, it revealed itself—a tattered curtain billowing slightly in a draft that seemed to originate from nowhere and everywhere at once. Anya reached out, touching the faded fabric. Its texture felt cool against her palm, and she was struck by the way it seemed to yearn for attention after years of neglect.

"What stories do you hide?" she whispered, somewhat aware of how silly it sounded. The curtain swayed slightly as if responding to her question, a gentle tease that sparked a sense of connection within her.

"Okay," she murmured to herself, trying to regain her composure. "Focus."

* * *

ANYA MOVED through the expansive foyer, letting her fingers brush along the worn banister with its intricate carvings. Each creak of the floorboards sent a ripple of anticipation up her spine, echoing the mansion's long history as if the very walls whispered secrets from a time long past. She glanced at the tapestries hanging crookedly on the walls—faded colors weaving stories of nobility, loss, and heartache.

Snippets of her imagination came alive, bringing to mind people who once walked these halls—laughing, crying, loving. She took a deep breath, the stale smell of old wood mixed with dust, reminding her that she was on hallowed ground.

"Okay, let's see what you're hiding," she murmured to herself, stepping into the shadowy embrace of the hallway that stretched beyond the foyer.

As Anya ventured deeper into the mansion, her heart raced, a spark of excitement mingling with the chill that snaked through the air. Her footsteps echoed softly, a reminder that she was alone, yet something nudged her forward, a magnetic pull urging her to uncover more.

Turning a corner, she spotted a tattered curtain, its faded fabric swaying gently as if inviting her closer. Curiosity piqued, she tugged it aside and discovered a narrow, winding staircase spiraling upwards into the gloom. A thrill shot through her—secret passages were the hallmarks of good stories, and she felt as if she'd stumbled into one of her own tales.

With each cautious step, the old wood creaked underfoot, as if protesting her ascent. She reached the top and faced a door that stood apart from the rest: worn, with edges softened by years of secrets held within. It beckoned her with a sort of tender caution, daring her to breach its threshold.

Anya took a deep breath and pushed it open.

The door creaked, and as it swung wide, sunlight flooded the dim corridor, illuminating a room where dust motes danced lazily in the air. She stepped inside, heart racing from the exhilaration of her discovery.

The sunlight spilled through tall, arched windows, casting a warm glow over the cluttered space. A mix of furniture dinged and worn, older than she could imagine, crowded the room, giving it a lived-in feel despite the years of silence. In the center, her gaze seized upon a table heaped with old trunks and wooden shelves crammed with books, their spines cracked and faded, as if they longed for eager hands to flip open their pages.

But it was the table that caught her breath, causing her to drop her bag onto the floor in her eagerness. An array of love letters sprawled across its surface, each piece adorned with elegant cursive—a testament to a passionate heart captured in ink. The ink faded, but the emotion emanated from each page, telling stories of yearning, longing, and the ache of unfulfilled desires. She picked up one letter, fingers trembling against the fragile, yellowed paper.

"Dearest Clara,"

It began, words echoing broken promises and affinity. The letter boasted phrases heavy with emotion, each word tugging at Anya's heart, as if the ghost of love itself lingered here.

Beside the letters lay an old, leather-bound notebook. Anya's breath hitched at the sight—an unfinished novel, its cover scuffed and soft. Papers poked out at awkward angles, yellowed and frayed like autumn leaves. She gingerly reached for it, cradling it in her hands as if it were a precious relic.

What were the chances? she thought, her heart swelling with a sense of possibility. She bit her lip, feeling a familiar mix of excitement and apprehension. *An unfinished novel when my own stands still at home?*

Her mind raced. This former resident, whoever he was, had left behind a treasure trove of emotions. Maybe, just maybe, these letters would spark inspiration for her own story. Maybe she could weave the threads of love and longing into her own tired pages.

Unexpectedly, a serendipitous sense of camaraderie bubbled inside her. She set down the notebook and traced her fingers over the elegant letters again, feeling the pulse of the love that had been poured into each one. A part of her wished to learn more about the people who had shared these words, to know their laughter and heartbreak entwined in the fabric of time.

"It's beautiful," Anya whispered, speaking more to the room than to herself. She couldn't help but smile, a warmth spreading through her despite the whispers of unease that had returned. This room, this hidden chamber, held echoes that resonated with her spirit.

She settled herself at the table, her heart racing. The unfinished novel drew her in further, its ink seeped with emotion, as if waiting for someone to breathe life back into its forgotten world. A treasure chest of stories and dreams lay at her fingertips, begging to be unraveled. Anya picked up the notebook, opening to the first page, the words—as vivid as dreams—leading her deeper into the voice of a long-gone author.

But the letters still called to her, whispering their longing and love, begging for reviving. The delicate entwining of both her desires and the spirits of those who had come before her ignited a fire within her once more. As she scanned the letters, her thoughts began to weave, liberated from the shackles of self-doubt that had plagued her back at home.

For this was it. Here, she wasn't alone. Here, the attic of secrets was filled with unrealized dreams and unfulfilled hearts, blending her existence with theirs. A stitch in time, binding her to the stories of love that stretched beyond her understanding.

As the sunlight poured in, illuminating the dust motes above like lost dreams, Anya made a silent promise to return and discover every secret contained in this sun-kissed room, reclaiming both their voices and hers.

3
the unsettling presence

As Anya rifled through the delicate love letters, the faded ink spoke of emotions long buried, stories of passion and longing that echoed within the walls of the mansion. She traced her fingers over the flowing script, imagining the hands that had penned each word, holding onto the dreams of a bygone era. The air in the room felt different—charged with the emotions captured within those fragile pages. Yet, among the romance flourished an unsettling chill creeping through the air.

A sudden gust of wind rushed through the hidden room, hinting at old secrets and buried fears. Anya's heart raced as a strange sensation prickled the back of her neck, like cold fingers trailing down her spine. The sunlight filtering through the window flickered, dimming briefly as if an unseen presence had passed, creating shifting shadows on the floor. She paused, her pulse quickening, and glanced around, her breath catching in a mix of excitement and fear.

This was her life—exposing the emotions of the departed, a daunting responsibility she had carried since she was six. Each visit from a ghost made her feel like a conduit, both embraced by their stories and burdened by their lingering regrets. She remembered her initial encounter with a ghost, a fragile apparition seeking resolution, its voice scarcely audible amidst the clamor of the mortal world. The sensations from that encounter—her heartbeat, her shivers—had eerily resurfaced within the confines of the mansion, reminding Anya of the light and shadows that danced around her.

"Come on, Anya. Just breathe," she muttered to herself, trying to regain her bearings.

But before she could collect her thoughts, the air shifted again, swirling with a force that felt almost tangible. The romantic atmosphere transformed abruptly into something electric. From within the mist, a figure slowly emerged, ethereal yet undeniably present. A young man took form, each movement fluid but with an otherworldly quality, like rippling water under the moonlight.

Anya stepped back, caught between the need to flee and the irresistible pull of curiosity. Her heart thudded against her ribs, and for an instant, she believed she had stepped into a dream, where reality blurred with fantasy.

With tousled dark brown hair framing his striking features, Eli stood before her. Those piercing blue eyes held her gaze, igniting an urgency within her. Whether it was the flicker of the lamps or the curious energy crackling between them, Anya felt every inch of her body aware of his presence. Here was the source of the unwelcome chill and the breath-taking anticipation.

"What…What is your name?" Anya managed to whisper, her voice almost swallowed by the tremors of the moment. A flurry of emotions boiled beneath the surface—fear, curiosity, something akin to awe.

"Eli Hawke," he replied, his voice smooth yet heavy with an eternity of longing.

Anya blinked in disbelief, trying to reconcile the reality of his existence with the weight of his words. Eli was more than a figment of her imagination; he was anchored in the here and now, hauntingly familiar yet profoundly distant.

"What do you want?" She tried to sound steady, though the quaver in her tone slipped past her guarded facade.

"You found my letters," Eli said with a hint of a smile, but his expression carried shadows of melancholy. "My unfinished tales." He gestured toward the sprawling collection of love letters littered across the table, their romance vibrant even in decay. "And my story, waiting to be breathed back to life."

Anya shifted her weight, nerves humming wildly. "You want me to write it?"

"Not just to write," Eli said, taking a step closer. The air thickened with tension. "But to understand it. To feel it." His voice softened, dripping with sincerity. "There's an emotional truth in those words, and you share that gift."

There was a weight to his gaze, one that grounded her but also left her feeling exposed. She swallowed hard, fighting against an urge to retreat, but somehow the notion of finding solace in his presence felt right. Here was a door opening—a pathway to something more than just secrets hidden in the past.

"Why me?" Anya asked, her voice barely above a whisper.

"Because you see things," Eli replied, shrugging off the weight of his own tragedy. "You understand. And I…" his voice faltered for just a fraction of a second, the longing lacing his words. "I need to finish my novel."

The plea in his eyes extinguished some of her panic, leaving a familiar spark of connection simmering in the air between them. But the intensity was overwhelming.

"What happened to you?" she blurted, the genuine curiosity rising as the pulse racing through her veins demanded answers.

Eli hesitated, the shadows flickering briefly across his features, reflecting a pain she couldn't yet grasp. "It's a tale of dreams unfulfilled. A life cut short." He took a deep breath, the ghostly figure becoming more ethereal than material, the air around him shimmering. "But I don't want to burden you with it now."

Anya's heart splintered with understanding, the darkness in his voice echoing in her chest. "I—I want to help," she stammered, even as a flood of uncertainty pushed against her resolve. Her hands trembled, caught between the love letters and the unfinished novel, but also in the face of his raw vulnerability.

Eli stepped closer, both a stranger and someone who felt like home. She could feel the air pulling them together, an unspoken bond wrapping around what she yearned to know and what she feared to uncover.

"Then stay," he urged, his voice low and inviting. "Help me finish this story, find closure together."

As the moment stretched, Anya's mind raced with thoughts. She couldn't ignore the questions coursing through her—was helping Eli a way to navigate her own emotions? Did she dare step, unshielded, into a story entwined with the past?

With a nervously bitten lip, Anya took in the gravity of Eli's request. The cool air wrapped around them, and she felt the quiet pulse of their connection.

* * *

ANYA STOOD FROZEN, heart pounding as she absorbed the reality unfolding before her. The air crackled with energy, drawing her in despite the shock coursing through her veins. Eli's ethereal figure loomed before her, his presence a mesmerizing blend of beauty and sorrow. A tremor of uncertainty jolted through her, but she couldn't turn away.

"Um, I—I'm Anya," she finally managed to whisper, her voice barely breaking through the charged silence.

Eli gazed at her, his piercing blue eyes piercing into her soul. "Anya." His voice slipped into the air like a soft melody, both haunting and bittersweet. "It suits you. I've waited so long for someone to come."

Anya shifted her weight from one foot to the other, caught between a strange exhilaration and an inching unease. She stared at Eli with wide eyes, the gravity of the moment anchoring her thoughts. "But… how long have you been— trapped in here?" Her question, though simple, felt heavy like a stone, weighing down the air around them. She studied him, seeking clues in his expression. The ethereal quality of his form flickered with sadness, and she felt a pang of empathy for this lost spirit who had been waiting on the other side of existence for so long.

"Over eighty years," Eli replied, his voice low, laced with an almost tangible ache. "I've been here since I died—trapped by the misunderstandings of everyone who's come after me." There was a softness in his gaze, an invitation to share his pain. "The previous owners thought I was haunting them, that I meant to bring terror. All I wanted was to be seen, to reach out. Some even gathered for séances, desperate attempts to rid themselves of what they thought was an unwanted spirit, but they never realized I wasn't there to scare anyone." Each word dripped with regret, echoing through the hidden room like an unresolved chorus. Anya felt the weight of his history, the loneliness of his existence, and an undeniable urge to help him find freedom washed over her.

Sorrow clouded his features as he continued, "I lived here once, a writer whose story was left unfinished when I… faded." He glanced at the scattered pages of his novel, laden with unfinished sentences and dashed hopes. "And my story," he trailed off, fingers brushing the leather cover, "remains trapped in time."

"What happened?" Anya's curiosity burned brightly, urging her to dig deeper.

"I was only eighteen when I died." He folded his arms, an all-too-human gesture of vulnerability overlaying his spectral form. "I had a life ahead of me, dreams to chase, stories to tell. But tragedy cut it short." A flicker of anguish passed over his face, leaving Anya with a sense of his unresolved pain.

She swallowed hard, empathy pooling in her heart. "That's… awful." Her voice trembled. "What do you want from me?"

Eli stepped closer, the air suddenly warmer between them. "I need your help, Anya." His expression shifted, intent and earnest. "You can see me—connect with me. You possess a gift that allows you to sense my despair and the stories waiting to be told. I want you to help me finish my novel."

Anya's breath caught in her throat, the request hanging heavy in the space between them. "Help you finish your novel? But I'm just a kid—a teenager," she protested, uncertainty clouding her mind. "I don't even know if I can write like you do."

"Your talent is already inside you," Eli breathed, hope kindling in his eyes. "You have a voice, a story that cries out for expression. I felt it the moment you stepped into this room. It's why I've been drawn to you. Together, we can bring my story back to life."

"But what if I can't? What if I mess it up?" Anya glanced at the faded pages piled on the table. The thought of tampering with Eli's legacy churned her stomach.

"Trust yourself." The way Eli spoke was almost magnetic, his sincerity crashing over her like a wave. "You're already here, in this mansion, destined to find me. You can help me uncover the truth, the love, the passion I poured into my work before life slipped away. But I need you to believe you can do this."

Anya felt heat bloom in her chest, mingling with fear. "What if—what if I fail you?"

Eli stepped back, the space between them heavy with tension. His eyes bore into hers, amplifying the connection they forged—a mix of yearning and desperation—pulling her into his world. "You won't, Anya. I promise." His voice, almost vulnerable now, layer by layer stripped away her hesitation. "Failure is what keeps me anchored here. I need closure, so I can finally move on. My story deserves a voice, and perhaps, so do you."

Compassion surged within her, overpowering her fear, rekindling the spark of inspiration that had dimmed for so long. She thought of her own unfinished stories, untold dreams that lived in quiet corners of her mind. "You really believe I can help?" she asked, her voice steadier now, hope infecting her words.

"I do." His expression softened, a genuine smile breaking through the veil of melancholy. It lit up his ghostly form, casting shadows that danced around them. For the first time, the weight of his sadness lifted slightly, revealing something complex beneath it—a shared vulnerability.

Anya sensed the bond blossoming between them, tethered by their mutual longing for expression—his for completeness, hers for connection. She felt compelled to bridge the gap, to help this charming spirit who resembled the night sky in his depth and mystery.

"Okay." Her voice held a determined steadiness that surprised even her. "I'll help you finish your novel."

Eli's eyes widened, an expression of pure gratitude sweeping across his features. "Thank you, Anya. You have no idea how much this means to me."

As the words hung in the air, Anya's heart raced. Behind her uncertainty lurked a thrill. She took a step closer to him, feeling the warmth of his presence wash over her, wrapping around her like a hug. "But where do we begin?"

Satisfaction glimmered in Eli's deep blue gaze. "Together, we'll delve into my manuscript. It holds the keys to unlocking my story—the love I lost, the dreams I clung to, the regrets that haunt me." He gestured to the table, the faded leather beckoning her closer.

Anya nodded, her heart fluttering with a mix of excitement and trepidation as she stepped toward the piles of history and emotion. The weight of Eli's story pressed upon her, both thrilling and daunting. She could feel the pull of the manuscript, but reality tugged at her conscience.

"I've got to go back now," she said, her voice tinged with reluctance. "My mother is probably wondering where I wandered off to. She worries, you know."

"You will return?" Eli asked, his anxious tone betraying a vulnerability that made Anya's chest tighten. His ethereal form seemed to flicker, as if her departure might cause him to fade away entirely.

"Yes," Anya answered without hesitation, her green eyes meeting his spectral gaze. "I'll be back tomorrow. I promise."

4
the weight of expectations

Anya sat at her rustic writing desk, the afternoon sun casting slanted beams across the scattered notebooks and loose papers that formed a nest of creativity—or perhaps chaos. A half-finished story lay sprawled before her, its pages crisp and blank, echoing her frustration. Though the remnants of Eli's unfinished novel rested next to her, its faded words taunted her with their lingering essence of lost dreams. She picked up her pen, twirling it nervously between her fingers, but the ink struggled to form even a single coherent thought on the page.

Every time Anya tried to write, her mind turned into a frozen tableau, paralyzed by nagging self-doubt. The vibrant ideas that had danced through her thoughts now faded into dull shadows, hiding in the corners of her consciousness. The house outside her window shimmered in the sunlight, the trees swaying gently, yet the world felt distant, as if muted by a gauzy haze. She turned her gaze inward, grappling with the storm of emotions swirling within her—fear, insecurity, longing, and guilt.

Frustration boiled over. With a sharp breath, Anya slammed her pen down but flinched at the sudden noise, sensing her distraction break the calm of her room. "What's wrong with me?" she muttered, her voice barely above a whisper. The silence that followed felt heavy, suffocating her thoughts.

Then, almost imperceptibly, the air shifted. Anya's breath caught, and she glanced to the side, her heart racing. Eli materialized beside her, his dark brown hair tousled, his piercing blue eyes bright yet tinged with something heavier—urgency, maybe?

"Hey," he said softly, a disarming smile flickering across his face that nonetheless sent a shiver down her spine. Anya couldn't help but feel both soothed and unnerved by his presence. *Had he followed her home, or had she simply summoned him in her distress?*

"Eli," she acknowledged, her voice cracking slightly, betraying the turmoil she struggled to mask. She looked away, unwilling to meet his expectant gaze.

He leaned casually against the edge of the desk, observing her with an intensity that made her pulse quicken. "Still not writing, huh?"

"It's not that easy," she snapped, surprising herself with the sudden edge in her tone. Bitter frustration spilled forth. "Your words are frozen on the page, Eli. They're…" Anya swallowed, searching for the right word but only finding more slippery emotions. "They're haunting me. What if I can't help you finish? What if I never find my voice?"

A flicker of annoyance crossed Eli's features, but he quickly masked it with understanding. "Look, I didn't mean to pressure you. I just thought—"

"Thought what? That you could magically inspire me or something? I'm not you." Her frustration morphed into vulnerability as she dropped her head into her hands. "You had this gift for weaving words, for creating worlds. I'm just a sixteen-year-old girl who can't even write one page without feeling like a fraud."

Eli stayed quiet, the air getting tense as he thought about her admission. Anya felt the pressure of his presence, a silent plea mixed in their shared space, telling her to see her worth. But his excitement about writing only made her feel more inadequate. She could feel the weight of his hopes on her, a burden she wanted to lift but was afraid she could never carry.

"Anya," he finally said, his voice steady and soft, drawing her attention back. "Every writer faces that wall—the doubt, the blockage, the fear of failing. It doesn't mean you aren't capable. It just means you're human."

"I'd argue that you're not," she mumbled under her breath, leaning back slightly in her chair.

Eli chuckled, his laughter warm yet carrying a touch of sadness. "Touché. But even I struggled, you know?"

"Really?" Anya blinked, her heart fluttering as she met his gaze. The sincerity in his eyes sent a thrill down her spine, igniting a flicker of hope within her. "What was it like for you?"

"Let's just say it involved a lot of scribbled notes, deleted lines, and the occasional existential crisis," he replied, brushing a hand through his hair, an endearing gesture. "I was consumed by the need to tell a story, and sometimes that can feel suffocating."

"But you overcame it," she stated, a hint of longing sliding into her tone. "You wrote…until you couldn't."

Eli's expression darkened, shadows weaving around him like the passing clouds outside. "Until life interrupted," he murmured, his voice growing heavy. "But every story matters. Yours especially, whether you can see it yet or not."

He leaned closer, forcing her to confront the warmth radiating from him, a stark contrast to her cold reality. "I'm not here to pressure you. I just want you to understand that writing takes time. It's okay to step back and breathe. Find something that inspires you."

In that moment, Anya felt both vulnerable and exposed. Eli's words pooled in the center of her being, combining with her own self-doubt like oil on water. She gazed at the faded novel on her desk, then back at his gentle expression, the weight of his lingering gaze igniting a heat she could not ignore. "I thought you'd bring me inspiration," she admitted, feeling the walls around her heart inch lower, exposing an uneasy truth.

Eli pursed his lips, a flicker of sadness dancing in his eyes. "Inspiration can come from different places. It doesn't always have to be me."

"No, it has to be you," she whispered, realizing the urgency underlying her words. Even as she acknowledged the cosmic nature of their connection, she hesitated to lay those feelings bare. "Your story…You deserve to be heard."

His gaze sharpened, every fiber of his being focused solely on her. "Then help me complete it. Write with me. We'd make a good team."

A soft breeze rustled through the window, tousling her hair and sending a shiver along her spine. Anya could feel the rich tapestry of possibility unfurling before her. The thought of working alongside Eli sent little flutters of excitement through her, but then doubt crept in like a cold fog. "What if I fail you?"

Eli's expression shifted, a hint of determination chasing away the shadows clouding his gaze. "I'll be here, every step. You won't fail. Together, we can breathe life into this story."

She glanced back to the unfinished pages, the scrawled ink whispering stories she yearned to uncover, both for herself and for Eli. Anya felt a stirring of courage within, nudged by a spark of inspiration ignited by their shared connection. With shaking hands, she cradled the pen again, a quiet determination settling in her chest.

"Okay," she breathed, allowing herself to be swept up in the narrative that unfolded between them. "Let's try."

* * *

ANYA SAT AT HER DESK, the pen poised above the blank page in front of her, trembling ever so slightly in her grip. Eli's presence swooped around her like a gentle wind, both comforting and disconcerting. He radiated an energy that both stoked a fire in her creative spirit and doused it in a wave of anxiety. She deeply felt the weight of their unresolved connection, intensifying into a storm within her.

As she stared at the pages of Eli's unfinished novel, she couldn't shake the thrilling yet terrifying attraction she harbored for him. Her mind flicked back to the fleeting moments of laughter they had shared—the spark in his blue eyes when he spoke about his passion for writing. It struck her as profoundly unfair; he couldn't exist in her world beyond these pages, yet here they were crafting something together.

"What if I lose myself trying to help you?" Her question hung in the thick air, laced with her vulnerability.

Eli sensed the tremors in her voice, and it stirred something in him, a mix of longing and regret. He moved closer, bending the space between them. "You won't lose yourself, Anya. Helping me could unlock something inside of you—a piece of yourself that's waiting to be discovered."

His words wrapped around her like a warm blanket, tempting her to embrace his plea. Still, doubts clawed at the edges of her thoughts. She pictured herself sinking deeper into the realm of the dead, giving up her tangible life for the abstract possibility of creativity unleashed. Suddenly, she worried about Jake, the boy from school who flashed her charming smiles and effortless charisma—the living warmth and connection she might be sacrificing.

"I barely understand my own abilities," Anya confessed, raising her eyes to meet his. "Sometimes it feels like a curse. It isolates me when all I want is to feel normal." Her heart raced as she uttered the words, a mix of fear and longing mingling within.

Eli's gaze softened. "You have a gift, Anya. The world you see, that couple with spirits and stories, it's beautiful." He paused, searching for the right words. "I know what it feels like to be trapped in fear. For me, it's about finishing my novel; for you, it's embracing who you are. Our journeys are intertwined."

Something flickered within her, a spark igniting in the quiet corners of doubt. Was it possible he could help her see her gifts as a path to self-acceptance rather than a burden?

But the sharp clang of reality pierced her reverie as she glanced around her cluttered room, the tangible reminders of her messy life making the space feel small and suffocating. "Eli, I'm scared. What if this connection leads me someplace I can't come back from?"

His expression deepened, shadows playing across his features as he reached out, his hand hovering just above hers, hesitant yet persistent. "I won't let you fall into a darkness you can't escape. There's comfort in the unknown, and we can navigate it together."

The air hummed with the unspoken weight of their shared experience, an understanding forming like an unbreakable bond. Though their worlds were fundamentally different—one bound to the ethereal and the other tethered to the living—they were both lost in their quests for completion and connection.

But the very thought made Anya shiver, a visceral reminder that each approach to the unknown came with its risks. "Eli, you're part of a world that's constantly slipping away from me. I can feel the allure of what we can create, but I also feel the emptiness—how I'm helping a ghost finish his journey while I'm left standing in the shadows."

Eli looked at her with a softness that pulled at her heart. "But every moment spent here with you fills the void of my existence. You're my chance to leave a mark on this world, Anya. Just like I'm a chance for you to find inspiration."

"If I say yes to this, then what does that mean for my life outside these walls?" Her voice trembled; she felt raw and exposed.

"The life you're living now is full of uncertainty, too," Eli countered gently, his tone woven with empathy. "Navigating the world as a medium is not easy, but it can lead to profound discoveries. What if working on my story could transform that uncertainty into clarity?"

At that moment, Anya felt the fragile threads of hope weaving their way into her heart, slowly untangling the fear she held. His words hinted at possibility—a world where she could accept her identity and merge it with the passion blooming between them. Yet clarity was an elusive dream, slipping further away the stronger her emotions became.

Taking a shaky breath, Anya shifted in her seat, struggling for stability as she locked eyes with Eli. "This could be more than just finishing your novel, you know? It feels like—like it might change everything."

"It might," Eli replied, his lips curving into a soft smile. "But if we embark on this journey, it demands commitment from both of us. You'll have to trust me, and I'll need you to trust yourself."

Anya swallowed, weighing his words. Trust had always been a complex terrain for her, especially with the shadows of her past lurking over her shoulder. With her internal conflict escalating, she knew she had to confront this rare opportunity to understand who she was and what her powers meant.

Moments passed as they held each other's gaze, the silence buzzing with tension. Anya felt that flicker of connection deepening into something urgent—a warmth blossoming amid her fears and uncertainties. The world slipped away, and all that remained was the intensity simmering in the air.

5
a glimpse into the past

dvor house

*A*nya sat cross-legged on the dusty wooden floor of the hidden room, surrounded by the love letters she had unearthed just hours earlier. The sunlight filtered through the window, casting a warm glow on the faded pages spread around her like delicate petals from a forgotten bouquet. Each letter felt like a history lesson, the elegant cursive capturing echoes of a time long gone. Curiosity fluttered in her stomach as she carefully unfolded one of the letters, her fingers trembling in anticipation.

The first line began with a flourish, the ink slightly faded but still rich.

> *"My Dearest Clara,"*

Anya's breath caught in her throat. These were the words of a man enveloped in passion, a man whose heart beat boldly on the pages before her. As she read through the intricate declarations of love, the ink seemed to breathe, drawing her further into the world Eli had once inhabited. He poured his soul onto each page, weaving tales of laughter, stolen glances, and moonlit rendezvous with the woman who captivated him.

With every letter, Anya felt herself slipping deeper into this bittersweet romance. She could almost hear the echo of Eli's laughter, see the way he must have grinned while crafting these words. The happiness spilled on the pages felt tangible, warming her heart, yet an undercurrent of sorrow ran through it all. The ink seemed to bleed uncertainty, an awareness of the fleeting nature of what was so fiercely cherished. Eli's longing was palpable, and she found herself charmed by the ardent spirit that danced through his words.

She reached for another letter, drawn to the romance that echoed her own life's desires. As she unfolded it, a rush of emotions flooded her senses—the smell of lilacs intertwined with the scent of old parchment, memories clinging tightly to each letter. The next lines narrated a vivid dream Eli had once whispered in the night.

"Together, we will write our destinies,"

Anya felt a pang in her heart. The words resonated with a deep-seated desire she had painted within her own pages—a longing for connection, for someone to share her ambitions and fears with. She also felt a growing connection to Eli; the dreams he chased, and the risks he took felt almost alive, whispering to her from the distance of time.

As she immersed herself in the letters, snippets of Eli's life unfurled around her. He had written about the dreams that danced beyond his reach, hopes that aligned with starry skies yet remained unfulfilled on Earth.

Distant friendships, laughter shared over cups of coffee, and youthful adventures leaped off the page, drawing her into scenes that felt strangely familiar. He wrote about warm summer evenings, the comforting warmth of companionship, and the shared ambition to create art that touched the soul.

And then there was Eliza—the name wrapped in warmth and affection, yet tinged with a profound sadness that Anya felt in her bones. She could sense how crucial she was to Eli's existence, how the thought of her lingered with him even in his final moments. Anya's heart ached as she grasped how deeply Eli had loved and how it had shaped him, driving him to write, to dream, to exist as a ghost bound by unwritten words.

With each passing letter, Anya faced herself in Eli's emotional landscape. Her own parallel stories surfaced—dreams that felt out of reach, relationships that left her longing for more, emotional walls built around her heart, similar to the defenses Eli must have erected to shield himself from the rawness of his pain. Flashes of her interactions with Jake flickered behind her eyes, memories tied to a boy who was undeniably alive yet found in moments of uncertainty.

She could almost hear Eli's thoughts mingling with her own, questions buzzing like restless gnats in her mind. *Would this love he cherished, bound to the past, overshadow any chance of a future? Did his ghostly existence keep him forever tied to grief, or was there beauty in those memories she hadn't yet discovered?*

"Anya," Eli's voice broke through her thoughts, gentle and haunting, sending shivers down her spine. She turned to find him hovering nearby, his dark hair flickering in the sunlight. He watched her with an expression that simultaneously held longing and an acceptance of the complexities surrounding them.

"I never shared those letters with anyone," he continued, his voice thick with emotion. "Not even her. They felt too sacred."

Anya's heart raced, caught between the weight of his past and the fragile space they now occupied. She sensed the sorrow and risks that came tethered to love—the treasures of vulnerability layered beneath layers of fear and loss.

"It's beautiful," Anya breathed, her eyes darting back to the letters. "I can feel how much you cared for her. How much you lost."

He closed the distance between them, the air charged with a pulsating energy. "She was my muse. She inspired me in ways I never understood until she was gone. I wish…I wish I had told her how deeply she moved me."

The words hung between them, heavy as the air in the room. Anya gripped the letter, feeling the weight of this connection. It transformed into a bridge between their hearts—but it also felt like a chain, binding them to their respective realms, living and spectral.

"What happened, Eli?" she whispered, vulnerability cracking her voice. "Did you tell her you loved her?"

Shadows flickered, and the atmosphere grew thick as she saw Eli's own regrets mirrored in his eyes.

"Not in time. I was too consumed by my ambitions, too afraid to expose my heart. By the time I realized…" His voice faltered, and the unfinished sentences felt like a weight on both their shoulders, the words begging for release yet refusing to break free.

Anya's chest tightened. She wanted to reach out, to bridge the gap that carried a history of love so profound yet marred by loss. Her heart ached not only for Eli but also for herself, her own battles pressing against her consciousness.

The bittersweet romance unfolded before her, layered with the beauty of love and the anguish of what lay unfulfilled. It echoed her own longings, dormant desires, and the haunting thought that she too might miss the moment to seize the connections that could define her.

As she kept going through the letters, a subtle sense of hope hovered nearby. Anya wished to write her own story—to complete what Eli couldn't—yet she understood that love required more than just words on a page.

* * *

ANYA LINGERED in the hidden room, sunlight filtering through the tall, arched window, illuminating the dust motes swirling in the air like tiny memories come to life. The love letters lay strewn across the table, each one whispering secrets and stories from a past that profoundly resonated with her. The bittersweet nature of Eli's lost love tugged at her heart, igniting an urge to share her discovery.

"Eli, are you there?" she called hesitantly, her voice echoing softly in the solitude of the room.

A moment hung heavy in the air before he appeared, materializing from the shadows like a gust of wind. Eli's ethereal form shimmered in the daylight, his piercing blue eyes alight with curiosity.

"What is it, Anya?" His tone was both eager and cautious as if he sensed the gravity of the moment.

"I've been reading the letters," she admitted, her gaze falling to the delicate pages. "You should see them. They're beautiful… and so full of heartache."

Eli stepped closer, drawn to the letters as if they held the key to unlock something deep within him. "You found them? Let's read them together," he urged, a flicker of hope crossing his face.

Anya picked up one of the letters, its edges worn and fragile. "This one… it's dated from just before…"

"Before everything changed," Eli finished, his voice dropping to barely a whisper, heavy with unspoken memories. The weight of nostalgia washed over him, palpable and raw. She began to read aloud, her voice steady yet soft, wrapping around the words as if giving life to the fading ink:

> *"My dearest, though the world may separate us, know that my heart beats only for you. The stars pale in comparison to the brilliance of your eyes, and I yearn for a time when we can be together once more."*

As Anya's voice filled the room, Eli's expression shifted. She glanced over at him, noticing the way his gaze turned distant, as if he were peering back into a past that felt both achingly familiar and painfully out of reach. She could see the heartbreak etched onto his features, the shadows flickering in the depths of his eyes.

"What happened to her?" Anya asked, her heart racing with empathy. "This woman you loved."

Eli swallowed hard, some invisible force drawing him into the gravity of their shared moment. "Her name was Clara," he said softly, memories swirling in his mind like autumn leaves in a brisk wind. "We fell in love that summer, but my dreams pulled me away, chasing stories and words. I don't think I ever told her how I truly felt… how terrified I was of losing what we had."

Anya reached out, her hand brushing against his. The touch was electric—a surge of energy that rippled through her as if the past whispered its secrets in their connection.

"How did you lose her?" she pressed gently, unable to mask the curiosity that egged her on. Eli's sorrow resonated too closely with her own fears, and she needed to understand.

"It was a foolish mistake," he admitted, his voice breaking slightly. "I let my ambition blind me. I didn't realize how much I needed her until it was too late. I never got the chance to tell her that I loved her."

A silence fell, thick with the weight of regret that hung between them. Anya felt her own heart twist at the confession, realizing the terror of letting love slip through her fingers. She thought of Jake, of the moments they had shared, but also of the distance that had quietly crept in between them.

"I've been struggling too," Anya confessed, breaking the silence. "I mean, not like you, but with my own feelings. There's Jake, who's so… real. But then you're here, and I can't help but feel this pull toward you. It's confusing."

Eli stepped back slightly, uncertainty flickering across his features. "But I'm just a ghost, Anya. You can't hold onto something that isn't really there." His voice was tinged with longing, and for a moment, the atmosphere thickened, heavy with unspoken possibilities.

"But we share something," she countered, urgency creeping into her words. "Your story… it matters to me. You matter to me." The admission echoed in the air, poignant and fragile.

"I don't want to be a complication in your life, caught in the space between your reality and my afterlife." Eli's expression hardened for a moment, as if bracing against the streak of vulnerability that coursed through him.

"But you are!" she replied, the intensity of her feelings spilling over. "You've opened up this whole other world for me—made me feel alive in ways I don't know how to explain. I want to help you finish your story, not just to ease my own burdens but because I feel something in this connection we have."

Eli's gaze softened, and in that instant, Anya felt the chasm between their realities flicker with possibility. They stood there, two souls woven together through threads of love and regret, not quite knowing where they would lead.

"You're brave, Anya," Eli said quietly. "For facing this… for wanting to dive deeper into what lies between us." He paused, his eyes searching hers. "But what would come of it? I could never want to hold you back from living while I remain trapped here."

"I don't know," she confessed, raw honesty spilling out. "Maybe it's about me discovering what love looks like, its beauty and its pain. Just like you… maybe we both need to understand how to let go while also holding onto something that matters."

Eli's breath caught in his throat, caught in the bittersweet weight of her words. "Then we do this together," he smiled faintly, a spark igniting within him. "Let's finish my story—together. Let's make it a tale worth telling, one that you can carry with you."

Anya nodded, her heart swelling with an unyielding hope as their fingers brushed together again, intertwining their fates as one. The air hummed around them, the heaviness of their confessions mingling with the possibility of shared journeys, fascinating and terrifying.

As they returned to the love letters and Eli's unfinished novel, a profound understanding bridged the lingering distance between them—a recognition that love, with all its imperfections, was worth every risk they might face. A bittersweet hope lingered between them, as if the very act of sharing their vulnerabilities had cast light into the darkness of their pasts and futures, illuminating a path forward against the odds.

6
moments of bonding

Anya settled into the worn armchair in the hidden room, feeling the comforting weight of Eli's presence beside her. Sunbeams filtered through the dusty window, illuminating the motes of dust dancing in the air, creating an almost magical atmosphere. In front of her lay Eli's unfinished novel, a faded leather-bound notebook filled with words that hadn't yet fulfilled their purpose.

"Okay," she started, her voice barely above a whisper. She bravely opened the notebook, the pages crackling in protest. "Let's see what you've got here."

Eli leaned closer, anticipation shimmering in his blue eyes. "Just… read the first few paragraphs. Just to start."

Anya turned a few pages, her heart racing with a mix of excitement and apprehension. The opening lines greeted her, words that felt alive yet trapped, longing for freedom.

"Once upon a time, beneath the light of a silver moon, there lived a girl with a heart full of dreams and a spirit bound by shadows…"

AS SHE READ ALOUD, the words came to life. The characters danced in her mind, vivid and compelling. Anya watched Eli's expression shift, his features animated as he listened intently, absorbing every word.

"That's… that's just the beginning," he murmured, a barely contained smile creeping across his face. "The protagonist's journey takes her deeper into a world where she must confront her deepest fears."

Anya paused, placing the notebook in her lap. "I can see why you never finished it—there's so much potential. But what if… what if the girl discovers a love that transcends time? One that not only challenges her but teaches her something about herself?"

Eli's eyes sparkled with enthusiasm, and he let out a low laugh. "That's exactly the kind of twist I needed! I had ideas, but you're adding a whole new dimension to it."

Bouncing from the chair with renewed energy, Anya grabbed a nearby notebook and opened it to a blank page. "Let's brainstorm! What does she need to confront along the way? Maybe a ghostly guardian who guides her?"

Eli leaned forward, excitement radiating through him. "Absolutely! And there could be moments when she doubts her own heart. The ghosts in her life—"

"—they represent the regrets she hasn't faced," Anya finished, scribbling furiously. She could hardly keep up with her thoughts, every idea seeming to spark another. "What if each ghost carries a lesson she has to learn? Each one reflects a fear, and she—"

"—has to unearth the true lesson behind each encounter," Eli interjected, his enthusiasm pulsing like electricity. "This will create a dynamic that evokes growth. She must actively learn and change!"

They exchanged ideas, laughter bubbling between them, ricocheting off the walls of the hidden room. Anya felt alive, energized by the creativity swirling in the air. It was as if her doubts faded away, replaced by a thrilling sense of possibility. It didn't matter that he was a ghost; in this moment, they were simply two passionate souls weaving tales together.

As the brainstorming session stretched on, Anya couldn't help but glance at Eli. He looked alive, vibrant, as if the world around him faded in favor of their shared creativity. Anya couldn't remember the last time she felt this way—so connected to another person, so in sync with someone else's dreams.

Eventually, they fell into a comfortable lull, scribbling notes and jotting down ideas. Anya set the notebook aside, resting her head against the chair, feeling overwhelmed but content.

"I can't believe we just did that," she said, a soft smile dancing on her lips.

Eli chuckled, shaking his head. "You're amazing. I never thought I could feel this way again, sharing my thoughts with someone. You have a gift, Anya."

She felt her cheeks warm, not entirely understanding why his compliment affected her so much. "Honestly, I didn't think I could write either. It's been hard for me. I often feel like I'm not good enough—like the words aren't worthy of existing."

Eli tilted his head, his expression shifting to one of sincere concern. "What do you mean?"

Anya hesitated, the weight of her insecurities pressing down on her. "Well, I don't know. It's like, everyone expects me to be this amazing medium, to help souls find peace. But when I sit down to write, everything falls apart. I can feel your passion, but I can't always tap into my own."

Eli's eyes held a knowing glimmer, as if he had sensed her struggle all along. "You know, when I was alive, I felt the same way. My father was a renowned playwright, and my mother was a poet. The pressure was immense. I felt like I had to live up to their legacy, which only made it harder to create."

Anya could see how this weighed on him, how his spirit bore the invisible scars of his past. "But you had a gift, Eli. You were already a writer. You just needed time."

"Time," Eli echoed, his voice heavy with reflection. "Time isn't something I got, and that's why it haunts me. I let my fear of failure keep me from writing what I truly felt. But, with *you*, I feel… liberated. Like there's a chance for redemption in completing this story."

The room filled with silence, and she met his gaze, a strange warmth wrapping around her heart. Here was a connection that was deepening in ways she never anticipated.

"What was she like?" Anya finally asked, uncertain but wanting to share this moment. "The girl you wrote about."

Eli's expression softened, nostalgia washing over his features. "Her name was Clara. She was vibrant, full of life and dreams she chased diligently. My feelings for her went unspoken until it was too late. It was one of my greatest regrets."

Anya felt a pang of sympathy for him. "You loved her."

"I did," Eli replied quietly. "But I wasn't brave enough to say it."

The atmosphere shifted, and Anya sensed the weight of his vulnerability settling between them, drawing her closer. "What about you, Anya? What do you dream of?"

She contemplated his question, her heart racing as she considered opening up the doors to her own insecurities. "I've always aspired to write my own book," she confessed. "But every time I put pen to paper, I freeze. I fear I won't do justice to my voice, or to the stories inside me."

Eli leaned forward, an earnest intensity illuminating his gaze. "You must trust your own voice, Anya. That's where the magic lies. It's okay to be afraid, but don't let fear define you. Your story matters, just like mine."

The sincerity in his voice sent a shiver down Anya's spine. They were kindred spirits, both tethered by their creativity yet weighed down by their individual fears. She could feel a pulse of connection, intertwining their experiences, bridging the gap separating the living from the dead, and in that moment, she began to reconcile her own dreams with her realities.

"I'll try," she said softly, her voice filled with resolve. "For both of us."

Eli smiled, a tender warmth spreading across his features that caught Anya's breath in her throat. Their laughter had faded, replaced by a charged silence filled with understanding and shared aspirations. In that dimly lit hidden room, among the ghosts of love letters and unfinished tales, something beautiful began to bloom between them.

* * *

ANYA LEANED against the wooden railing of the porch, her heart fluttering with excitement as she recounted her plans for the weekend. The late afternoon sun cast a warm glow over the overgrown garden, illuminating the vibrant wildflowers that struggled for attention amidst the tangled weeds. She now felt at ease with the mansion, the shadows of its interior no longer felt suffocating. Instead, they tinted her surroundings with a sense of wonder.

"I swear, he's like a breath of fresh air," she said, her smile wide as she described Jake's easy-going nature to Eli. "We talked about everything yesterday, from our favorite movies to the stupidest things we've done at school. You should've seen the way he made me laugh."

Eli sat across from her, perched against the edge of the porch, his form flickering slightly as the sun dipped lower in the sky, casting elongated shadows. His usual playful demeanor seemed muted, the warmth of the moment dampened by a growing unease.

"Sounds like a perfect day," Eli replied, his voice steadier than he felt. He attempted to mask the tightness in his chest, a mix of jealousy and a fear he couldn't quite articulate. It wasn't that he wished for Anya to be unhappy; he just wanted her to look in his direction when she spoke of connections.

Anya continued, animatedly recounting details, her green eyes sparkling in the fading light. She reminisced about the way Jake's laughter rang like music in the air, how he effortlessly made light of even the heaviest subjects.

"I never thought I could enjoy a simple day so much," she continued, blissfully unaware of the tension brewing in Eli's silence. "It's like he gets me in a way that feels... special."

The air trembled with an intensity that felt foreign, the comfortable banter between them shifting into murky territory. Eli's heart sank, a knot tightening in his throat. He couldn't hold the words back anymore.

"Do you really have to go out with him?" Eli's voice wavered, and the weight of his question hung thick in the air. The playful tone was gone, replaced by something raw.

Anya halted, her laughter evaporating into confusion. "What do you mean?"

Eli's blue eyes darkened, reflecting landscapes of emotion—anger, vulnerability, and fear. "You know what I mean. You talk about him like... like he's the only one that matters. Don't you see what's happening here?"

Her brows furrowed, an uncertainty creeping into her expression. "Eli, I—"

"I'm not trying to be jealous," he interrupted, frustration bubbling. "It's just—" He swiped a hand through his hair, a futile gesture, but the sweeping motion was loaded with urgency. "You're living; you have a life out there. And I'm just a ghost. It just feels wrong."

Anya shifted in her seat, the unease prickling her skin. "Eli, I—"

"You want to go out with him," Eli said sharply, his voice escalating. "You're excited about it. Meanwhile, I'm here, stuck, watching you make plans with someone who can touch you, who can hold your hand."

"Eli!" she exclaimed, her voice raised to counter his sudden conflict. "You're being unfair. I mean, I didn't plan this to hurt you. You know I care about you. You're... you're here with me; how can I forget that?"

"Forget?" Eli barked a bitter laugh, steeped in sadness. "You think I want you to forget? I don't want you to forget!" He took a halting step toward her, an almost desperate movement, trying to bridge the intangible distance that seemed to grow between them. "I just don't want to see you drift away!"

Anya's heart pounded, confusion twisting itself into knots in her stomach. She didn't know where to place her feelings. "But I can't ignore a connection just because you're... you," she whispered, a sharp edge of pain wrapping around her words. "I'm still figuring this all out, Eli."

"I'm not asking for you to ignore anything." His voice grew softer, but the frustration lingered, like an unattended fire smoldering just beneath the surface. "I'm asking for you to acknowledge it. It's not just about you having fun with him. I'm right here, Anya. I'm not gone. I—"

"Eli," she interrupted, her voice quieter now, filled with both compassion and uncertainty. "This is a lot for me to process. I... I didn't realize how you felt."

He stepped back, realizing the gravity of his emotions; they twisted within him like a whip crack. "You don't realize, do you? What this all means for me?"

Caught off guard, Anya struggled to center her thoughts, their conversation forging paths through her mind. She felt a ghostly weight draping over her, one that felt achingly familiar. "It's complicated. I can't just shut down everything with Jake because we have... this."

"Why not?" Eli's voice flared again, tinged with desperation. "Because it's easy to pretend? To ignore the truth? I care about you, Anya—"

"I care about you too, but you're… you're not alive!"

The revelation flared like a lightning bolt between them. Silence enveloped them, the sound of crickets filling the once-vibrant air with an eerie lull. Anya cringed, the weight of her own words felt merciless.

Eli's expression shifted, vulnerability eclipsing the anger. His frustration faltered, revealing a sorrow that lay deeper than she'd ever seen. "I know that," he murmured, his voice trembling, "but I don't want to lose you. I didn't ask for these feelings, and I sure didn't ask to complicate your life."

Anya felt her breath catch in her throat, her heart aching for him. The depth of his emotions nearly overwhelmed her, rooting her to the porch as the walls of the mansion creaked softly around them. "Eli, I…"

But the words fell short, tangled in a web of anxiety and scrutiny. The air between them seemed heavy and unyielding, as unresolved tension transformed into a chasm she didn't know how to navigate.

As the evening sun sank below the horizon, a chill settled in, reminding them both of the challenges ahead. Eli took a step back, leaving a gap that lingered in the air between them.

7
creative breakthrough

The morning light filtered through the dusty windowpanes of the hidden room, casting an ethereal glow on the scattered papers strewn across the table. Anya sat in her usual spot, pen in hand, but the words that usually flowed so freely now evaded her. A sense of helplessness washed over her, the weight of writer's block pressing down like a heavy blanket. She dropped the pen with a frustrated sigh, its clattering sound echoing in the silence, amplifying her distress.

Eli's presence seemed to materialize from the very essence of the room. His airy form hovered near the doorway, brow furrowed in concern, which stirred a mix of warmth and anxiety in Anya. She wished for his comfort but also felt the tension from their previous conversation still hanging like a specter between them.

"Hey," Eli said, his voice soft yet encouraging. "You seem… stuck?"

Anya leaned back in her chair, shaking her head as if that would somehow clear away the chaos in her mind. "I can't focus. It's like my thoughts are trapped behind a brick wall." She gestured at the cluttered table, papers filled with scratchy notes and half-formed ideas. "I thought writing would help me make sense of everything, but all it does is remind me how lost I feel."

Eli stepped closer, his expression shifting from concern to a glimmer of excitement. "Maybe we need a new approach," he suggested, giving her an eager smile. "Let's brainstorm together. You know, like a writing exercise."

"A brainstorming session?" Anya raised an eyebrow, intrigued yet apprehensive at the idea. Would doing something different help? The prospect of collaborating with Eli ignited a flicker of hope.

"Yeah!" Eli's enthusiasm burst forth like sunlight breaking through clouds. "We can take turns prompting each other. It'll push both of us to think outside the box. Plus, I want to hear you read your pieces aloud. I know how much your voice brings the words to life."

Anya considered his proposal. The thought of sharing her thoughts with Eli brought an unexpected thrill that overshadowed her apprehension. "Alright," she agreed, her pulse quickening at the idea of this fresh dynamic between them. "Let's do it."

They settled into their new rhythm, playing off each other's energy. Eli suggested the first prompt, leaning against the table and glancing at her with a mischievous sparkle in his blue eyes. "How about…" He paused for dramatic effect, lips curving into a sly smile. "Write about the moment two lovers lock eyes across a crowded room, and the world fades away."

Anya's pen lifted eagerly, her hand moving almost instinctively. With Eli's words swirling in her mind, she began to write, letting her imagination sweep her away. The sensations flooded back with each stroke of the pen. She painted the scene with vivid detail, feeling the heat of the lovers' gaze and the palpable tension that ensued. "In that crowded room, their eyes met, and suddenly, everything else vanished—the loud chatter, the clinking glasses, even the faint music playing in the background. It was just them, wrapped in an invisible thread weaving their hearts together."

As she read the passage aloud, Eli leaned in closer, his breath hitching ever so slightly, revealing his fascination.

"Keep going," Eli grinned, his features brightening in the glow of her words. "You're onto something here."

The encouragement sparked a newfound confidence within Anya. "Okay, your turn," she said, her excitement bubbling.

"Alright." Eli rubbed his hands together like a child about to dig into a pile of candy. "Let's switch gears to something more whimsical. Write about a secret garden where the flowers can talk."

Anya jotted down the new prompt, wrapping her mind around the concept of a hidden world teeming with character. She penned a vivid scene, picturing vibrant blooms bursting with life. With each line, she could almost hear the chatter between the petals, playful secrets shared on breezy afternoons.

"Did you know?" one flower gossiped. "That sunlight isn't just for us? It's like a gift—we can feel the warmth and it makes us bloom brighter!"

They both laughed, the sound reverberating in the room like a joyful melody. It was infectious, the kind of laughter that lifted spirits, diluting the remnants of tension that had once loomed over them.

Eli's eyes sparkled with delight as he leaned closer, momentarily losing himself in the imagery of Anya's words. "You have a gift, Anya. No one else can paint worlds like you do."

Blushing at his praise, she felt his admiration warm her chest. With fresh inspiration filling her, she leaned forward as he proposed another prompt—a series of quick ideas, layers of imagination unfolding between them. Each prompt built on the last, a wave of creativity igniting in the space they shared.

Eli would look over while she wrote, adding intensity to the moment. Sometimes, he would lean in, his breath barely a whisper, sending tingling thrills through her as he offered suggestions, balancing guidance with simply enjoying her presence.

"Remember to weave in the threads of my story," he encouraged once, his voice low. "The essence of longing, of facing the past. It can add a deeper dimension to your narrative."

Anya nodded, her mind swirling with the connections between their stories. The weight of blending their experiences coursed through her fingers like electricity. She wrote, entwining elements from both their lives, expressing their emotions through the fictional lens they were creating together.

With each triumphant word, she could feel the hesitations dissipating, the entanglement of their thoughts becoming a reflection of their connection. As time passed, the gloomy shadows of her writer's block began to lift, revealing the vibrant colors of creativity and collaboration.

"Look at us," Eli said with a soft chuckle, his eyes filled with warmth. "Two writers slowly unraveling our stories in this dusty corner of a haunted mansion."

Anya caught his gaze and grinned, her heart racing a little faster. "Who knew a ghost could be so useful?" Their exchange felt effortless, and the playful banter began to feel more comfortable, more natural.

As they delved deeper into their collaborative dance, the emotional walls separating them slowly crumbled, reconfiguring the space they occupied. Anya noticed how he seemed to draw closer each time she shared her thoughts—a tangible magnetism that left her breathless.

The flow of ideas spilled into laughter, ideas blossoming into an involved tapestry of interconnected creativity. Both writers thrived in the safe embrace of shared ambition and mutual respect, fueling each other's fire. Anya, fueled by Eli's spirited approach, found that her fingers seemed to dance across the page. She read her pieces aloud with growing confidence, each laugh they shared another thread weaving their hearts a little tighter.

"Maybe we're onto something great here," Eli murmured one afternoon, excitement electrifying the air around them.

Anya smiled, feeling the thrill of their combined creativity rush through her. The magic of the moment filled her, quelling the fears that had once plagued her.

"Definitely," she agreed, her heart warming at the prospect of their burgeoning connection. Their collaboration had unlocked more than just words—it had ignited an evolving bond slowly forming from the echoes of their intertwined narratives.

As the afternoon sun began to sink beyond the horizon, Anya breathed in deeper, letting the comforting sense of creativity envelop her like a warm hug. It was a feeling she never wanted to lose.

* * *

ANYA'S DAYS at Dvor House settled into a unique rhythm, one that intertwined her writing sessions with moments of unexpected camaraderie with Eli. Each afternoon, the hidden room became their haven, a sanctuary where stories flowed and laughter danced in the air like the dust motes illuminated by the warm sunlight streaming through the windows.

As they worked together, an unspoken bond began to thrive in the little moments of connection they shared. The playful banter came easily, words bouncing back and forth like a favorite game. Anya would roll her eyes at his teasing remarks about her character choices, her laughter ringing out like music in the hushed space.

"Seriously, your protagonist has more angst than an orchestra filled with teenagers," Eli declared one day, mischief sparkling in his piercing blue eyes.

Anya shoved his shoulder, her own eyes alight with playful indignation. "At least my character isn't a ghost who can't figure out how to finish his own story."

Eli's laughter mixed with hers, the sound filling the room with a buoyant energy. She glanced up and caught a lingering gaze from him, his expression softening, the teasing fading to something more genuine. It made her heart race. It was a complicated feeling, a wild mix of delight and confusion that left her breathless.

Their exchanges began to shift, subtle yet electrifying. Anya felt her cheeks heat when Eli leaned closer, his breath brushing against her skin as he read over her shoulder, the warmth transferring to her like an unspoken promise. Moments where their hands brushed against one another became frequent, brief but poignant, a spark igniting a thrilling tension that pulsed steadily beneath the surface.

One afternoon, the air in the room seemed to shimmer with anticipation. Anya had just crafted a piece inspired by Eli's past, a heartfelt scene that walked the line between tragedy and beauty.

With every word, she channeled the bittersweet essence of their shared experiences—an intimacy that resonated with her own blossoming feelings. When she finished reading aloud, she looked up to find Eli's expression transformed, a mixture of longing and hope flickering in his eyes.

"I never knew you could capture my past with such… beauty," Eli murmured, his tone rich with emotion. The gravity of his words pulled Anya in, and she felt a warmth bloom in her chest as their gazes locked.

"Just like you inspire me," she replied, a teasing lilt to her voice that disguised the rush of feelings swirling inside her. "Next time, maybe you can give me a prompt that doesn't involve a tragic ghost."

Eli leaned in closer, their faces inches apart, and whispered with mock seriousness, "But you're missing out on all the fun, Anya. Tragic ghosts have so many stories to tell."

Her heart raced, the air around them crackling like a charged storm. Emboldened, Anya decided to push the boundaries a bit further, teasing him about his ghostly nature. "True, but your invisible tendencies might scare away my other potential characters."

The playful banter erupted into laughter, but suddenly the mood shifted. Eli's fingers skimmed along the surface of the table, hesitating just before brushing against hers. The physical contact lingered, an electric jolt that sent a shiver down her spine. The laughter fell away, replaced by a heavy silence, and the intensity between them deepened, infusing the air with unspoken emotions they both tried to navigate.

Anya caught her breath, feeling weightless in the moment. She gazed into Eli's eyes, where a world of raw vulnerability lay hidden beneath his confident facade. In that instance, the line between friend and something more blurred, leaving her breathless and yearning. The gravity of their feelings hung over them, palpable and thrilling.

Eli hesitated, a flicker of uncertainty dancing across his features. Anya could see his struggle clearly—a ghost bound to the remnants of his past, grappling with feelings that transcended life itself. The moment stretched, taunting them with the challenge of embracing something neither of them had expected to find.

"Anya," Eli finally broke the silence, his voice low and sincere. "You're… you're not afraid of me, are you?"

Anya's breath caught in her throat. She shook her head slowly, looking up at him. "No, it's not that…"

"Then what is it?" His tone held a quiet urgency, searching her for answers.

"It's just… complicated," she admitted, her pulse racing. The truth hung there, a weight they both felt, as Eli's gaze intensified, drawing her in deeper.

"I know," he replied, his voice barely a whisper yet filled with conviction. "But complications can lead to beautiful things, don't you think?"

His words wrapped around her, stirring a fire deep within that blurred the lines between trepidation and desire. Anya swallowed hard, her heart pounding in response to the longing that blossomed between them. She couldn't deny the allure of what could be, despite the boundaries set by their vastly different worlds.

With a breath that trembled in her chest, Anya squeezed his hand, a tentative reassurance. "Maybe," she replied, a hint of a challenge in her tone.

Then, without knowing why, she leaned in closer, their breaths mingling, sensing a powerful connection brewing. Eli's eyes darkened, an emotion flickering across his face—hope entwined with uncertainty. In that moment, Anya was acutely aware of everything—the warmth of his skin, the magnetic pull between them, and the weight of their entwined fates lingering in the room's charged atmosphere.

8
growing affections

Anya sat at a small table on the café's patio, soaking in the golden rays of the sun that warmed her skin. Laughter floated around her, blending with the lively chatter of nearby patrons. A gentle breeze shuffled the leaves of the tree overhead, casting flickering shadows that danced across their table. She took a sip of her iced tea, the sweet citrus flavor refreshing against the back of her throat.

Jake leaned back in his chair, a wide grin spreading across his face as he animatedly described his latest skateboarding mishap. His sandy hair caught the light as he motioned, illustrating how he'd misjudged a jump and ended up tumbling to the ground, his laughter ringing out like music. Anya appreciated how easy it was to be with him—he had a way of making the world feel lighter, like the weight of her thoughts about Eli melted away under his warmth.

"So, did you manage to flip your board back around or did you just flail about like a fish?" Anya teased, playfully raising an eyebrow as she took another sip.

Jake chuckled, feigning offense. "I'll have you know that I'm an expert flailer. One of my many talents."

Their laughter bounced between them, filling the air with a sense of intimacy that felt new and exhilarating. As they swapped stories and snacks—a shared plate of fries between them—Anya noticed the way Jake's hazel eyes sparkled with genuine interest. He hung on her words as she recounted her recent adventures exploring Dvor House, intrigued by the layers of history she uncovered in the hidden room.

"You seriously have to give me a full tour of that haunted mansion," he said, leaning forward, his elbows resting on the table. "I have so many follow-up questions! Are there actually ghosts? Do they try to scare you? Or do they just chill? Like, 'Hey Anya, how's it going?'" He mimicked a casual ghost voice, his playful inflection sending Anya into another fit of laughter.

She felt warmth bloom in her chest, excitement surging through her. It was refreshing, being here with Jake. They could joke about the supernatural, and for a moment, it made her forget the complexities of her connection with Eli. Yet, her mind wandered back briefly to the mansion. Did Eli watch her from afar, feeling the same pang of jealousy that sometimes crept into her thoughts?

"Of course, I believe in ghosts! At least, one particular one," Anya said, forcing herself to sound light-hearted as she tried to shake off that lingering thought. "But I'm pretty sure he's not the chill type."

Jake's eyebrows shot up, feigning surprise. "Oh really? So, I'll need to prepare for a haunted adventure? Should I bring my ghost-busting equipment? Just in case?"

"Definitely. There may or may not be ectoplasmic residue. Who knows what we might face?" She picked up a fry and waved it in front of him, and they both dissolved into laughter again. The world felt buoyant and bright, the sunlight glowing like them, amplifying every shared glance and smile.

As the conversation flowed, Anya felt more alive than she had in weeks. Jake's playful compliments about her writing elicited shy smiles. "You really should publish something, Anya. You have a way with words."

She felt a flutter in her stomach at his sincerity, wondering if it was too bold of her to admit how much his encouragement meant. For countless nights, her writer's block had stifled her creativity, and yet here Jake was, making her see her talent anew.

"What about you, Mr. Keller?" Anya leaned in, intrigued. "Do you have any hidden talents?"

"Only all the coolest skills," he declared dramatically. "Like mastering the perfect dad joke." He paused for effect, then delivered a groan-worthy pun about falling off a skateboard. As Anya attempted to suppress her laughter, she reveled in the effortless chemistry sparking between them. It felt intoxicating, their banter weaving a web of potential that left her heart racing.

"Okay, okay, that was truly terrible," she admitted, eyes sparkling. "But I like it! I might just have to record your dad jokes in my journal for posterity."

"Just think, one day when I'm super famous, you can say you knew me before I became a legend," he replied, and leaned so close she could see the little freckles across his nose. The teasing glimmer in his eyes contrasted sharply with the warmth blooming in her chest.

Anya's cheeks flushed, the moment stretching between them like a tightrope. Her breath caught when their hands brushed against each other, a simple touch that sent a rush of electricity coursing through her. For that brief moment, the busy café faded into the background—the laughter and chatter around them receded into a soft hum, leaving just the two of them suspended in their own world.

"Believe me, you're definitely going to be a legend," she said softly, and her heart thumped louder than the café's music.

The playful atmosphere shifted slightly, taking on a more intimate tone. Jake shifted closer, his voice dropping to a conspiratorial whisper, "So, seriously, have you ever seen any ghosts? I'd be totally terrified."

"Maybe," she said, unable to suppress a coy smile, feeling like she was stepping into dangerous territory. She enjoyed stirring that curiosity in him while battling the echo of Eli's presence in her mind. "I might have… one in particular who seems to be a pretty good writer."

"Wait, you're telling me he's a ghostwriter?!" His laughter exploded, drawing the attention of a few nearby tables. Anya bit her lip to stifle her giggles, knowing that her heart raced for more than just the joke.

"Just what I needed! Ghostwriting puns about ghostwriters," she said, shaking her head in mock annoyance as they rocked back and forth in laughter.

Jake locked his gaze with hers, something deeper flickering between them that made her pulse quicken. "I'm down for a ghost tour anytime, but I swear if I hear any poltergeist stories, I'm outta there! You know I freak easily."

"You'll be fine. Just hold my hand," she teased, but the weight of sincerity fled into the very air that surrounded them. That brief playful invitation twisted in her gut, creating a yearning that mingled dangerously with the memories of Eli.

"Deal," Jake said, his voice low and edged with a hint of something more.

Just then, the café door swung open with a creak, and the breeze carried a familiar scent of blooming flowers mixed with aged wood—an unmistakable whisper of the mansion. Anya's heart skipped as a wave of emotion washed over her; she felt large, steady eyes regard her from the depths of her mind, Eli's presence looming like an uninvited storm.

"Wanna take a walk?" Jake asked, quickly following her gaze.

"Sure, in a moment." The humor faded on her lips, her heart wavering. The moment stretched, mixing lightness and heaviness.

Jake's hand lingered just above hers, electricity curling between them as he leaned even closer, watching her with a patient intensity. "What's going on in that head of yours? You look like you just lost a game of chess."

Anya fought against the urge to look away, knowing the truth tangled within her emotions, inching toward revelation. Both men captured her heart's attention, yet she couldn't ignore the pull of the past threatening to unravel everything she'd found in the moment.

* * *

ANYA STEPPED through the doorway of Dvor Mansion, the familiar creak of the heavy door echoing in the vast silence. The air felt different, charged, as if the very walls were holding their breath. She dropped her bag by the entrance, her thoughts still swirling with the laughter and warmth she had shared with Jake just hours earlier. The sunlight streamed through the tall windows, illuminating dust particles that danced in the stillness.

"Eli?" she called out, her voice barely rising above the whisper of the wind outside.

He materialized from the shadows, leaning against the wall with an unreadable expression. His typical carefree aura had shifted into something darker, tension knotting his features. Anya's heart skipped a beat, feeling the weight of his gaze. Eli's piercing blue eyes flickered with a storm of emotions that pulled at her insides —confusion, longing, and something else she couldn't quite place.

"Hey! You won't believe what happened!" Anya exclaimed, her voice brightening with excitement. She stepped closer, eager to share details about the café, the laughter, and the way Jake's hazel eyes lit up when he smiled.

Eli's posture remained stiff, his arms crossed tightly over his chest. "What did you do?" His voice echoed off the high ceilings, laced with an edge that sent a shiver down Anya's spine.

She faltered, her smile fading slightly. "Um, just grabbed some coffee with Jake. He was really sweet, and we talked about… well, everything. He even said he wants to come by and check out the mansion."

At her words, Eli's expression darkened, his jaw tightening. The spark of jealousy flared in his eyes, and Anya felt heat rise in her cheeks, a mix of guilt and annoyance curling in her stomach.

"Why do you keep seeing him?" Eli's voice dropped, each word intentionally pronounced, as if cutting through an invisible line separating the living from the dead.

"What do you mean?" Anya countered, bewildered. "He's just a friend. We were hanging out."

"Just a friend?" Eli's laugh was sharp, devoid of humor. "You think that's what this is? Just a friendly little coffee date?" He pushed himself away from the wall, moving toward her with an intensity that made the air thrum.

Anya took a step back, a sudden rush of confusion flooding her. "Eli, you're not being fair!"

"Fair?" he repeated, his voice rising. "Do you think it's fair that I'm here, tethered to this place, while you're out living your life? Do you have any idea how that feels?"

She felt her heart race, the tension in the room suffocating. "You don't get to dictate who I can be friends with, or who I can spend time with!" Her own voice surged, the frustration spilling over, making her feel vulnerable yet defiant.

"I'm not trying to dictate! I'm trying to—"

Eli's anger surged as he clasped his hands, and suddenly, a gust of wind swept through the room, rattling a stack of books on the nearby table. Anya's breath hitched; the air grew colder as objects began to shift, floating slightly in defiance of gravity. A chair slid across the floor in a dramatic display, impacting against the wall with a loud bang.

"Eli, stop!" Anya cried, feeling a deep, visceral fear at the display of his power in anger. "You can't just scare me like that! I'm just trying to understand!"

"Understand what?" Eli shot back, frustration licking at the edges of his words. "Understand that I can't just watch you grow closer to someone else? That I'm stuck here, unable to reach out or hold you?"

His voice cracked, revealing the raw pain woven into his frustration. Anya's heart ached in response, feeling the tumult of emotions churning within him. She longed to reach out, to bridge the distance that had suddenly widened between them, yet the fear of his hurt pushed her further away.

"You can't expect me to stop living my life because you… you're gone, Eli!" Anya's eyes glistened with unshed tears, her voice thick with emotion. "I want to help you, but I can't do that if I isolate myself from everyone else!"

He paused, breathless. The room fell silent, the only sound was the quiet drumming of her heart. Eli's expression shifted, sorrow replacing anger. "You don't understand. I get it—I really do. You're young, and there's so much out there for you. But… I'm scared. Scared of losing you to someone who can touch you, who can hold you."

Anya's defenses faltered as his vulnerability struck her. She hadn't anticipated this side of Eli, the softening of his intensity revealing the fragile human beneath the ghostly visage. "Eli…," she began, her words faltering, unsure how to bridge the emotional chasm between them.

He took a step closer, his breath mingling with the charged air, weighing her next words with urgency. "Sometimes I feel like I'm fighting for something I can never have. That you'll forget me the moment you find someone new."

The gravity of his words sent an ache through her chest, highlighting the complexity of their connection. Anya wanted to comfort him, to reassure him that she wouldn't forget. Yet, her own heart resonated with confusion. "It's— it's not like that, Eli. I—"

But before she could finish, the air between them thickened, an invisible barrier reflected by Eli's uncertainty. He turned away abruptly, fingers brushing against the edge of the table, and in an impulsive burst of energy, the scattered papers soared into the air, swirling like a gentle storm before crashing down again.

Anya stood frozen, a mix of awe and fear at his control over this reflection of his turmoil. "Eli, please, don't do this—" she began again, but he interrupted her with fierce passion, the emotions running raw and unchecked.

"Why do you keep going back to him?!"

"Because I can," she stated, her frustration pounding against her chest. "For so long, I felt trapped by my abilities to connect with the dead. I thought being friends with you meant I had to shut everyone else out. But I can't do that. Not anymore."

Eli turned slowly to meet her gaze, desperation flickering in his eyes. "You're choosing him over me," he whispered, the hurt in his tone palpable.

"I'm not choosing! I want to be a part of both worlds, Eli!" Anya's voice cracked, her cheeks hot with unshed tears. "I don't want to lose you—I care about you. This isn't about choosing Jake or you. I'm trying to figure out where I belong. I thought we were figuring this out together."

Eli looked as if she'd struck a chord deep within him. His face slumped, and she could see him wrestling with the reality of their situation. The juxtaposition of their emotions wove a fracture in the room, a gap that felt insurmountable.

Anya suddenly felt a sense of loss, as if the walls of the mansion were closing in on her. The bond she'd cherished between Eli and herself now felt strained, their connection threatened by the presence of Jake.

The silence stretched painfully, heavy and unyielding. They stood on opposing sides, their unresolved feelings hanging in the air like the tension before a storm. Anya felt lost, and Eli seemed to embody every ghostly reminder of the regrets they shared.

9
uncovering the truth

Anya paced the dusty floor of Dvor Mansion, her mind a whirlpool of confusion after the confrontation with Eli. The air felt thick with unresolved tensions, each breath heavy with the weight of their unspoken words. She needed clarity—an escape from the chaos stirred within her heart. Shifting her focus away from the tangled emotions regarding Eli and Jake, she decided to immerse herself in the mysteries of the mansion.

As she roamed through the dim hallways, a flicker of determination ignited within her. Anya was drawn to the promise of secrets waiting to be uncovered, each corner of the house whispering stories that clamored for her attention. The creak of the floorboards accompanied her as she ventured deeper into the house, curiosity guiding her steps. Her fingers brushed along the wallpaper, peeling in places, a tactile reminder of the history wrapped around her.

The grand parlor stood heavy with silence, the shadows casting abstract shapes on the walls. Anya gripped the doorknob to a small door next to the fireplace. Pushing it open, she entered a forgotten room cluttered with dusty furniture and cobwebs. The musty air caressed her skin, a blend of nostalgia and age.

Anya rummaged through old trunks, box after box filled with a jumbled assortment of faded memories. Most items were mundane—yellowed photographs, tarnished silverware, and moth-eaten clothes—but in the back of her mind, she held out hope for something more, something that might connect her to the spirit she had grown to care for.

While she organized the scattered remnants of the past, her gaze landed on a large trunk locked tightly with rusted hinges. Intrigued, Anya knelt before it, searching for a way to pry it open. The trunk seemed imbued with an aura of secrecy, and her heart raced as she considered the possibility of revealing something deeply personal.

After scraping together some strength, she managed to leverage a sturdy old candlestick against the lock. The trunk creaked open unexpectedly, as if it had been waiting for years to be disturbed. Inside lay an assortment of journals, their leather covers worn, alongside a few delicate keepsakes cocooned in mothball-scented cloth.

Anya's hands trembled as she picked up the first journal. The pages were lined with familiar handwriting—Eli's neat, flowing script. A sense of reverence washed over her as she flipped through the entries, the intimate thoughts of the young man she'd begun to know cracking open like a treasure trove. The very soul of Eli seemed to breathe through the words, each stroke of the pen revealing pieces of his heart.

She settled into a corner of the musty room, her eyes scanning the delicate page edges tinged with gold. The entries took her back to a time when Eli was alive, painting a picture of a young man filled with hopes and dreams, yet laden with the weight of emotional scars.

Days turned into weeks in the journals, documenting moments of joy mutated by the shadows of despair. The entries revealed a tumultuous relationship with a woman named Clara, filled with tender declarations that pulsated with a fierce love unable to shield them from the struggles of life. Each turn of phrase dealt with the fragile nature of human emotions, the highs and lows of romance colliding with reality.

But as Anya continued to read, the tone of Eli's writing shifted, tinged with anguish. Her pulse quickened as she reached a chilling entry dated just days before his death. Eli penned his thoughts with raw honesty, recounting a night that changed everything—a night he had failed to protect Clara. The words sank into Anya like a stone dropped into a still pond, sending ripples of dread through her.

"I could have saved her,"

he wrote,

"but I was too late... I stood frozen, paralyzed by the thought of what might happen. I should have known better. My inaction stole her life."

Anya's breath hitched, regret clawing at her insides. Eli's guilt radiated from the pages, intertwining with the pain that seeped into every line he had written. She clutched the journal tightly, her heart racing as the enormity of his emotional ties bore down on her. With each carefully penned word, Anya felt herself tangled in a web of understanding. Eli was not just a charming ghost longing for companionship; he was a tragic figure, weighed down by layers of pain that became increasingly visible.

The next journal entry was an echo of despair.

"I will never forgive myself,"

Eli had scrawled, his frustration pouring over the edges of the page.

"I was supposed to be her protector. Instead, I left her to face the darkness alone."

Anya's heart ached for him. A whirlpool of empathy churned within her, forcing her to confront her feelings about Eli—not just as the ghost she was growing close to, but as a person who bore scars she now understood. How could she reconcile her budding attraction to him with the anguish that shaped him? Every word threatened to unravel her emotions, complicating the affection she had nurtured, leaving her in tumult.

Staggered by the weight of Eli's burdens, she closed the journal, letting the air catch her breath. Her mind raced, grappling with the reality that Eli's unfinished novel didn't just reside in the pages of his writings; it thrived in the moments he had shared with her, laced with the intricate interplay of love, loss, and regret. Eli was standing at a crossroads, desperate for closure that she hadn't realized was weighing him down.

Beside the journals lay a small heart-shaped locket, dulled with age. Anya picked it up, her fingers lingering on its surface as her mind filled with questions. *Who had it belonged to? Had it belonged to Clara, the person who haunted Eli's memories?* A tight knot formed in her stomach; with every discovery she made, the connection to Eli grew deeper, but so did the realization that their paths were dotted with shadows—his past wounds and her own uncertainties.

As she placed the locket back inside the trunk, heavy thoughts swirled in her mind. Anya leaned back against the trunk, absorbing the revelations. Strands of air in the room felt charged, like they were straining against an invisible current. She could sense Eli nearby; despite his absence, the tangled emotions lingered heavily like a fog, threatening to envelop her.

With the journals ultimately prompting more questions than answers, Anya took a deep breath. She understood now that discovering Eli's secrets was just the beginning of understanding the complexity of her feelings. The secrets of the past haunted the walls of Dvor Mansion, whispers echoing in the shadows around her, but it was the emotions that intertwined with those whispers that she needed to confront. And as she left the hidden room, a realization dawned on her—this was just the beginning of unraveling their entwined tales, for better or worse.

* * *

AS THE EVENING DEEPENED, shadows deepened in the hidden room, wrapping around Eli like a shroud. Anya stood at the entrance, her heart thundering in her chest. The air felt heavy, laden with the things left unspoken, the fears that stirred like phantoms in her mind. She felt the journals tucked under her arm, their weight an uneasy reminder of the secrets she had uncovered.

Eli lifted his gaze, his piercing blue eyes searching hers. There was an instinctive understanding that flickered between them, a tension laden with anticipation. Anya hesitated, her thoughts racing.

"Anya?" His voice broke the silence, laced with concern. "What's wrong?"

Taking a breath, she stepped further into the room, the door creaking softly behind her. "I found your journals."

A flash of surprise crossed his face, quickly becoming a mask of dread. "You did?"

She unfolded one of the worn pages slowly, each word a revelation that had felt like a betrayal to Eli's fragile spirit. "I read about your past... about her. Your lost love, Clara."

He clenched his jaw, the vulnerability washing away his curiosity, revealing a dark shadow of turmoil etched across his features. "I didn't want you to know. It's not a story for you." His voice hardened, a barrier slamming down between them.

"But it is a part of you," Anya pressed. "Why can't you see that? Understanding it helps me understand you!"

The silence deepened, heavy like the thick tapestry of shadows around them. Eli's gaze turned inward as he wrestled with emotions he thought long buried. "I wanted you to know me," he murmured, almost to himself. "Not the ghost with regrets."

Anya's pulse quickened, a knot tightening in her stomach. "But how can I separate the two? Your past is a part of your story. It's intertwined with your heart."

"I'm not just a tragic memory," he retorted, frustration etched into his features. "I refuse to be defined by that."

She shook her head, feeling tears prick her eyes. "I know you're more than that. In fact, you're vibrant and alive in a way that's so rare. But hearing about the guilt you carry… it breaks my heart, Eli."

His expression shifted, the walls he'd built around his feelings beginning to tremble. "You think I wanted this weight to linger over me? I just wanted to be a writer. To create things worth remembering."

"But you are," she insisted, stepping closer, unable to keep the longing from her voice. The connection she felt with him was undeniable, stemming from their shared passion, their whispered moments of creativity. "I want to help you finish your novel because I care about you, all of you. Past included."

For a moment, vulnerability flickered across Eli's face, his defenses wavering. "Caring isn't easy, Anya. It's complicated."

"I know," she whispered, emotions swirling through her like a tempest. "But I'm trying. I'm creating too, and I don't want to lose that ability, or you, trying to shield you from your past. Maybe we both need to confront it."

His gaze softened, the shadows in the room dissipating slightly, yet the tension remained. "You don't know what you're asking. You can still walk away, Anya. I'm… I'm saying goodbye to my life every day."

Anya's heart raced with urgency and weighty understanding. "But I don't want to leave you behind. It's not fair, Eli! Can't you see—"

"What about Jake?" The question slipped from his lips, sharp and biting. A raw edge coursed through his voice, pain reflecting like a razor through their moment.

Anya hesitated, a myriad of emotions clashing within her. "Jake's different. He's the living, breathing world I've kept at arm's length, and it's comfortable. But with you…"

"Is that it?" Eli interrupted, frustration radiating from him. "Is it easier to play with ghosts than confront someone real? Am I just a distraction?"

"No!" she exclaimed, her voice a mix of desperation and hurt. "You're so much more than that. You inspire me. Both of you — in different ways. But it scares me, Eli."

Eli's shoulders slumped slightly, a flicker of uncertainty crossing his features as the vulnerability crept back in. "I'm scared too. I keep hoping you'll choose me, that maybe I can be someone worth your risk. But every time you smile with him… it twists like a knife."

Anya swallowed hard, feeling the weight of their rapidly deepening connection standing in stark contrast to her burgeoning feelings for Jake. "I don't want you to suffer."

"I don't want to suffer either, but I can't be a ghost forever," Eli replied, anguish lurking just beneath the surface. "That past… it suffocates me, and I've tried to push it away, but it feels like it's all I have now."

Tears pooled in Anya's eyes, her heart aching for the battle he faced, not only against the perception of others but against his very existence. "Eli, I want to be part of your future, but we need to confront these secrets together. You deserve to let go."

His eyes danced with hope and fear, the lines of his throat tightening as he considered her words. "Together?"

"Yes," Anya affirmed, feeling a flicker of determination rise within her. "I want us to create our truths. Your story is not just a collection of regrets, but it can be a bridge to new beginnings."

Eli stepped closer, their connection tangible, yet still fraught with uncertainty. "And if I can't forget? What if I remain trapped in this?"

"Then we'll explore it together," Anya responded, resolved to bridge the gaps between their worlds. "Let me help you finish your story, whatever it takes. I'll bear the weight of this with you."

Eli's expression softened, hope gleaming from the depths of his gaze as he reached for her hand, their fingers brushing gently. The tension hung in the air, thick with the emotions that wrapped around them like an unbreakable thread.

Anya stood frozen in the hidden room, Eli's presence lingering like a fragile thread connecting her to two contrasting worlds. Each heartbeat echoed in her chest, the weight of her burgeoning feelings making her dizzy. She couldn't deny the allure of Eli—the way his laughter flowed like music, the depth in his blue eyes that mirrored her own tugging emotions, and that undeniable spark of creativity they fostered together. With every word they shared, every brush of his hand against hers, a warmth ignited within. Yet as she glanced at the fading sunlight filtering through the window, a flicker of doubt crept in. Could she honestly embrace this budding romance, knowing she had something real with Jake? The thrill of being grounded in a living connection clashed violently with her growing attachment to a ghost whose very nature pulled them apart.

Her thoughts spiraled as memories of Jake rushed forward to compete for her affection. Jake was the sun-drenched reality—his laughter infectious, his charm undeniable. He was vibrant and alive, everything she had ever imagined when dreaming of a high school crush. The way he looked at her ignited butterflies within, making her feel seen in a way that was new and exhilarating. Yet, with his face fresh in her mind, Anya struggled to grasp the significance of the electric connection with Eli. She wanted to lose herself in his stories, to see beyond the tragic lines of his unfinished novel. But those moments felt so dangerously escapist, leading her toward a realm shrouded in whispers of sorrow and yearning, where she could only carry so much weight without crumbling. A longing tugged at her heart, a battle brewing between the allure of embracing Eli's ethereal world and the desire to be anchored by Jake's warm embrace.

Anya felt torn—how could she reconcile these feelings? Each day that slipped by deepened this internal struggle, and the closer she grew to Eli through their collaboration, the more painful it became to disregard her feelings for Jake. The pull to explore her unknown connection with Eli mixed with the crushing guilt of neglecting her bond with Jake. Neither boy deserved the confusion swirling around her heart. She shifted her gaze back to Eli, whose expression mirrored a mix of hope and apprehension. She sensed that he held his breath, waiting for her reaction, seeking reassurance that they could truly navigate the stormy seas between them. The air felt thick, charged with unspoken words that could either transcend their boundaries or doom them to remain perpetually confined. Would she have to make a choice between ghostly inspiration and radiant affection? Anya's heart ached with the realization that she might soon need to confront the truth she had avoided for too long.

10
a quiet reflection

The flickering light barely illuminated the corners of the hidden room, casting dancing shadows that swirled about the walls. Anya sat cross-legged on the floor, notebook cradled in her lap, staring at the unfinished manuscript of Eli's story. The yellowed pages swam with untold tales, a bittersweet reminder of a life that had ended too soon. The earlier conversation hung like a storm cloud above her—her heart a battleground between her growing feelings for Jake and the intense connection she felt with Eli.

The atmosphere felt heavy, infused with whispers of the love letters strewn around the room, their intimate words echoing in her mind. She felt Eli's presence in the air, lingering at the edges of her thoughts, while the ghostly shadows flickered and danced, reflecting the tumult within her. On one hand, Eli's passion for storytelling ignited a fire in her soul. But, on the other hand, Jake's laughter rang in her memory—warm and inviting—reminding her of the comfort she craved amidst the turbulence of her emotions.

She closed her eyes for a moment, inhaling the musty scent of age—papers and secrets long kept hidden. It felt like a breach in time, a bridge between her vibrant world and the spectral realm that Eli inhabited. But Jake represented everything alive—possibilities, laughter, and a normal life. Here, in the mansion where she now had one foot in the afterlife, Anya found herself utterly torn.

Without the slightest warning, Eli materialized near her, a specter emerging from the shadows. The soft hues lighting up his familiar features made him appear almost real, but the slight shimmering around his form pulled her back to the harsh truth of his existence. He approached slowly, his expression one of cautious concern, and the tension hanging in the room thickened as he recognized the weight of her internal struggle.

"Anya," he murmured, his voice lightly echoing in the stillness. "What weighs on your heart?"

She bit her lip, searching for words that felt elusive, and then finally, they spilled forth. "I want to help you with your novel, Eli. I truly do." Her eyes fell on the manuscript again, yearning to uncover its secrets, to breathe life back into the pages. "But there's Jake," she continued, feeling vulnerable as the truth rolled off her tongue. "He makes me feel... seen. Alive."

Eli's gaze flickered with intrigue and a hint of sympathy, as if he could see the fragility in Anya's emotions. "Love and friendship... They can be intertwined," he began, his tone shifting toward deeper reflection. "But they also come with the weight of sacrifice. Sometimes, we have to choose one path over another."

Anya swallowed hard, the gravity of his words settling like stones in her stomach. She nodded, feeling the flickers of joy and sadness battling within her. "I want to complete your story, Eli. I want to help you find closure."

Eli stepped closer, a mixture of affection and pain evident on his face. "I understand how hard it is to slip away from connections made in life," he said softly. His piercing blue eyes bore into hers, the weight of a profound understanding wrapped in every word he spoke. "But being true to yourself and your heart… that is not a betrayal. It's a beautiful risk, Anya."

"I just don't know how to balance it," she admitted, feeling raw and unguarded. The truth spilled from her heart, a flood of emotions threatening to overwhelm her.

Eli moved to sit beside her on the floor, their nearness amplifying the palpable tension. "Pursuing love can lead to heartbreak, but it can also lead to the most incredible moments. There's beauty in taking those risks; it's what makes life worth living… or even un-living," he added, his voice laced with a sorrowful humor that echoed long-buried pain.

Anya leaned into him, despite the ethereal boundary that separated them, wanting nothing more than to comfort him while seeking solace in return. "I feel drawn to both of you," she confessed, her voice cracking. "Jake… he's real, he's *here*, and we have fun together. But you—what we share is so deep. It's like… it's like writing poetry without even knowing what the words mean."

An electric silence enveloped them as Eli considered her words, and she could see the conflict ripple across his face. "Sometimes, we don't need to fully understand something to feel it," he replied, sincerity threading through his voice. "You're tapping into something profound, Anya. You're writing your own story at the same time as being part of mine, and that's important."

Anya pondered this, her fingers absently tracing the edges of Eli's manuscript. The connection between them felt like rhythm, a verse building toward something deeper. Yet, buried underneath was the complexity of what it meant to create two lives intertwined in such starkly different worlds—one vibrant with laughter, the other shrouded in melancholy.

"I want to be there for you, Eli," Anya whispered, her heart aching for the ghost beside her. "But I can't ignore the happiness I feel with Jake either. It feels... unfair."

"Life is often unfair," Eli replied, a shadow of sadness crossing his face. "But perhaps what you're feeling isn't a burden. Maybe it's an opportunity." His voice was warm yet edged with tension. "You can carry both connections with you. A lightness can be paired with heaviness, and joy and sorrow can coexist."

As Anya listened, her heart raced. The intimacy between her and Eli deepened in an unexpected way—her soul resonating with his truths. The lines between her emotions grew blurred, yet illuminated by his understanding; it felt both liberating and unnerving.

Instead of fear, she felt a flicker of hope ignite within her—a sense that it was possible to embrace both worlds—to be the bridge connecting them without placing limitations on her heart. She allowed her mind to wander, questioning if love, in all its forms, could truly fill the voids that life had created.

"I want to write your ending, Eli," Anya said, the resolve washing over her like a warm embrace. "But I don't want to close a chapter of my own in the process."

Eli's warm gaze met hers, the turmoil ebbing for the briefest moment. "Then let's take this journey together," he proposed, a hint of determination softening his features. "Your story matters, Anya. Don't forget that."

* * *

WITH THE WEIGHT of unsaid words hanging in the air, Anya took a deep breath, her voice trembling as she confessed her fears. "I can't help but think… if we finish your novel, you'd be gone. You'd leave me behind." Her green eyes glistened with unshed tears, reflecting the turmoil she felt—a mixture of longing, confusion, and dread.

Eli's expression softened, a warmth radiating from his being. He reached out, not in a bid to comfort her physically, but instead, the essence of his presence enveloped her. "Anya," he said slowly, his voice thick with emotion. "Love isn't about keeping someone with you. It's about allowing them to be free. If we complete my story, it won't erase what we've shared. It will give me peace, and you… you can live your life."

The words sliced through Anya, igniting something deep inside her. She understood this intellectually, but acceptance proved another battlefield entirely. "But how can I be happy with Jake knowing that…" She hesitated, the truth stinging her throat, "You'll be gone?"

Eli stepped closer, his blue eyes piercing through the haze of uncertainty. "I want you to be happy, Anya. That means embracing the living. I can't cling to you. I can't hold you back from love." His voice wavered a moment, revealing the depth of his struggle. "You don't have to sacrifice anything. Helping me find closure doesn't mean we must lose what we have. It's just a different kind of love."

A heaviness settled in Anya's chest, filled with equal parts dread and confusion. "But how can I let you go? How can I move forward in a world without you in it?" *Oh, she gone and done it. Expressed her true feelings.* The fight inside her grew more intense; a battle between the ethereal connection she cherished with Eli and the burgeoning relationship she shared with Jake.

"Moving forward doesn't mean forgetting," Eli responded, his tone earnest. "We've created something special together. The stories will remain in you. They'll inspire you, just as you've inspired me. Love is not bound by time, Anya. It transcends everything. You have so much life left to live."

She recoiled slightly at his words, anguish twisting inside her. "And what if I don't want to forget? What if I want this… us, to mean something more?"

Eli's brow furrowed, pain dancing across his features. "By holding on too tightly, you may lose everything. Please, if you truly care for me, let me go." He leaned closer, his voice barely above a whisper. "I want you to have every happiness life has to offer… including a future with Jake."

The mention of Jake felt like a sudden jab to Anya's heart. Memories surfaced—the warmth of Jake's laughter, the sweet gestures he extended that made her feel alive. Yet here stood Eli, every moment they shared present in the air between them, the ties they forged in creativity and the invisible threads of emotion binding them even tighter. "I don't know if I can," she breathed, feeling her resolve begin to crumble.

The energy in the room shifted, crackling like static electricity as their hearts laid bare in the dim light. Eli opened his mouth to speak, hesitating a moment, searching for the words. "I don't want you to feel trapped. You deserve so much more than the specter of my existence. Every moment we spent together has mattered more than you could ever know. But there's a clock ticking for both of us. I am a ghost, Anya, caught between worlds." His voice cracked like fragile glass threatening to shatter.

The tears finally spilled over, cascading down Anya's cheeks. "I feel torn between this incredible bond I share with you and this incredible boy who brings me joy. It's like I'm betraying you by choosing him."

"Choosing happiness isn't a betrayal; it's honoring what we've shared," Eli insisted, his voice rising to meet her anguish. "Look at me." When she dared to meet his gaze, he continued, "You deserve love that you can feel, touch, hold tight. I lost my chance to create those memories. Don't lose yours."

Their eyes locked, a sea of emotions crashing between them—fear, longing, and an undeniable connection woven from shared moments that felt sacred and transient all at once. As Anya felt the tug of her heartstrings—one part yearning for freedom and the other clinging desperately to the persona she had come to know in Eli—she realized how monumentally heavy her choice would be.

"Eli, I'm scared." Anya's voice cracked, her breathing ragged. "I don't know how to go on without you." The vulnerability of her confession stripped away any remnants of bravado, leaving her vulnerable and exposed.

"I'm not leaving because I want to. I'm leaving because I have to." Eli's voice trembled slightly, revealing the tension of his own dilemma. He stepped forward, closing the distance that felt like a chasm when she most needed him to bridge it. "Don't mistake my departure for a lack of love, Anya. It means I love you enough to let you fly, even if it means I watch from the shadows."

"You just want me to forget you," she argued, new waves of desperation clawing at her heart. The thought of letting go threatened everything she had begun to feel—an absolute, aching terror filled her chest.

"Never," Eli promised, his gaze intense with sincerity. "But you have to live for yourself. You can't spend your life bound to a story yet unwritten. Your life is the story now. Finish my tale, set me free, and I'll always be with you in spirit, as your muse, your inspiration."

In that moment, something clicked for Anya. The weight of Eli's words settled into her heart, igniting a spark of hope within her. He could be her muse, her strength as she navigated the landscapes of creativity and the chaos of emotions entwined with loss. "I can finish your story," she whispered, an unexpected rush of determination coursing through her veins.

With that thought pushing her forward, she envisioned Eli's unfinished novel—a tale woven with threads of love, longing, and, ultimately, the tragedy that marked his life. The faint smell of the old journal mingled with the dust in the room and filled her senses, grounding her in the present moment. Anya's heart raced, not with fear or sadness, but with a burgeoning excitement. She could weave his narrative and plunge herself into the depths of creation, etching Eli's story into the world as a tribute to the passion that blossomed between them.

"Online," she said, feeling renewed confidence take root. "I can publish it online." The idea unfurled in her mind like a flower bursting into bloom, each petal revealing another layer of possibility. "If I finish it, I can share it with anyone willing to read. It won't remain lost forever. It would be out there."

Eli's eyes widened, a flicker of hope igniting within their depths. "You really think people would read it?" His voice was tinged with disbelief, mingling with excitement. "Who would care about a ghost's story?"

"A lot of people," Anya asserted, her spirit unfurling like a flag catching the wind. "There are tons of stories out there about love and loss. Yours is unique. And I won't just finish it for you—I'll put it out into the world." The conviction in her statement took her by surprise, as if she were tapping into a deeper resolve she hadn't yet recognized.

The thought spun in her mind, a whirlwind of inspiration and ambition. Many writers had gained success through self-publishing in the digital age, their words resonating across borders and generations. *What if, just what if*, Clara, Eli's first love, might stumble upon it? She must be in her eighties now, a life lived on the fringes of Eli's lost existence. Perhaps she was still alive, still searching for remnants of the past, waiting for the echoes of a love story buried under years of silence.

Anya's heart pounded. Surely Clara might see it. The weight of the thought filled her with fervor—if there was even the slightest chance Clara could hear about the love Eli had for her, then it was worth the effort. It rang like a bell, resonating within her. Every letter Anya had read from the past blended with the warmth of Eli's energy beside her, and she felt connected to a time long gone, bridging gaps between their lives.

"Can you imagine, Eli?" she exclaimed softly, lost in her daydream. "What if it gets noticed? What if Clara reads it—that she finds comfort in your words? She would finally know how much you treasured her."

A smile stretched across Eli's face, reflecting a mix of disbelief and joy that lit up the shadowy corners of the hidden room. The tension of their earlier conversation began to dissipate, replaced by an infectious hope. "If Clara could read it… that would mean everything," he admitted. "It could provide a sense of closure for me."

"Exactly," Anya emphasized, her excitement punctuated with enthusiasm. "We'll finish your novel together—your immortal legacy. We can do this." Her mind started racing through the myriad of ideas still swirling chaotically. She could work tirelessly day and night, fine-tuning every word in those yellowed pages, pouring herself into Eli's unfinished tale, cultivating it into something beautiful that would leave a mark on the world.

Eli leaned in closer, intrigued. "What do you think will happen once it's out there? Do you think it could reach her?" His gaze seemed to drift slightly, peering beyond the room and the mansion, envisioning a world outside where stories breathed and connected people, transcending the boundaries of time and space.

"Why not? The online world is so vast. People share stories constantly—there's a community of readers waiting for something real, something raw." Anya's enthusiasm echoed off the walls as she started to envision a plan, creating a checklist in her mind. "I could use social media, create a blog… maybe even connect with some local writing groups. We could spark interest. Clara could discover it or hear about it through someone."

Eli's eyes glimmered with a mixture of longing and hope, making the space between them almost tangible. "That's incredible, Anya," he murmured, the weight of his emotions softened as he recognized the possibilities blooming in her mind. "It goes beyond me, doesn't it? It could capture not just my story but your voice and passion as well."

"Exactly. I want my voice to resonate along with yours. Your experiences, your heart—it all matters." Anya's words flowed with conviction, swimming through the air like a song that wrapped around them. "I'll make sure the world knows who you were, and maybe, just maybe Clara could find solace in knowing you loved her endlessly."

The spark of a plan began to ignite in Anya's heart—a tangible project that provided a bridge to untie the knots of grief and longing. The weight of Eli's world became lighter against the horizon of her ambitions. They stood on the precipice together, ready to create something that could resonate through the years, a love letter to the past that might just find its way back to its tender roots.

Eli's expression changed, the brief flicker of doubt replaced by growing excitement. "Then we have work to do," he said, a grin breaking across his face. "Let's get started."

11
the blog

Anya sat cross-legged in the sunlit parlor of Dvor House, sunlight streaming through the cracked leaded glass, casting dappled shadows on the worn mahogany floor. Her fingers hovered hesitantly over her laptop's keys, a half-finished cup of tea steaming beside her, the faint scent of chamomile competing with the musty smell of old books. The air felt thick with inspiration, but also with a weight that pressed against her chest.

In the corner of the room lay a stack of Eli's love letters, their faded ink a testament to aspirations and heartaches. She needed to write, to share the world Eli had opened up for her, but the pressure to do justice to his story loomed like a shadow. Anya had been wrestling with her emotions, her thoughts a tangled mess, but now, as she glanced at the letters, a spark ignited within her.

She reached out for one of the letters, the delicate paper brittle under her fingers. Unfolding it carefully, she immersed herself in the melodious cadence of Eli's words: passionate, aching, alive. As she read, the essence of his longing seeped into her heart, and

Anya could feel the burn of words stirring to life beneath her fingertips.

With a surge of determination, she turned to her laptop, the anticipation thrumming in the air around her. As she began typing, words flowed like a river breaking free of its banks. Each sentence stitched together the narrative of Eli and Clara—a story intertwined with warmth and heartache, nostalgia, and unfinished dreams. The title formed in her mind:

"Letters of Longing: The Love Story of Eli and Clara."

The scene shifted in her mind as she delved deeper into this world, crafting their romance against the backdrop of Dvor House. She wrote about moonlit promises exchanged in hushed whispers and the stolen glances that ignited flames of passion. Anya highlighted not just their love but the heartbreaking reality of time stolen away, mingled with the urgency of creations left incomplete. Eli's emotions danced on the pages, and she breathed life into Clara's story through her words.

Hours slipped by unnoticed as the adrenaline surged through her veins, fueling her resolve. It felt intoxicating to share someone else's private heartache, to weave her own creativity into the fabric of Eli's story. And as she typed the final words, a sense of satisfaction settled over her like a warm blanket.

With a deep breath, Anya hit "publish." Her heart raced, uncertainty surging alongside exhilaration. She leaned back in her chair, staring at the screen as the words clouded her thoughts. It felt different—the blog had always been a personal refuge for her scribbles, a place to share fragments of her life. *But this?* This felt monumental.

Waves of apprehension chased the excitement through her blood. *What would her readers think? Would they truly connect with Eli's pain? Might they judge her understanding of love, of loss?* She hesitated for only a moment before sharing the link across her social media platforms. A flurry of butterflies filled her stomach as notifications lit up her screen, almost instantly.

DAYS TURNED into a whirlwind of activity as likes began to trickle in, then flood. Notifications popped up like fireflies against the encroaching night. Each ding echoed like a heartbeat, growing louder and more vibrant as new comments and shares materialized. Anya was overwhelmed; her modest audience had transformed into something dynamic and alive, a connection she never anticipated.

Praise flooded in, her words sparking conversations and resonating deeply with people. "Beautifully written," one commenter wrote, while another expressed, "This story is so relatable." As Anya scrolled through the approving responses, her chest swelled with pride. She was touching hearts, sharing the weight of emotions that transcended time. In the rush of validation, there was a simmering sense of responsibility settling over her—her words mattered. They bridged the living with Eli's lingering spirit.

Yet beneath the euphoria, a creeping self-doubt threatened her elation. *What if she misinterpreted Eli's story? What if she clinched onto fragments of his experience, twisting it into something that might never reflect the truth?*

Somewhere between the third and fourth cup of tea, Anya's mind drifted momentarily away from the anxiety that plagued her. That's when she saw it—a chilling notification twisting the joyful anticipation in her stomach.

A message from someone with an unfamiliar name flickered on her screen,

> "I think I know Clara. This story belongs to my family."

Her heart plummeted. A knot of anxiety curled in the pit of her stomach. *What did this mean?* Instinctively, she hesitated, her fingers hovering over the keyboard. Uncertainty flashed, colliding with her fervent curiosity. *Who was this person? What would they reveal about Eli—or Clara?* The implications spun in her mind like a whirlwind, and she couldn't shake the feeling that everything she had pieced together might suddenly shatter.

Should she respond?

Anya felt the thrill of discovery gripping her heart tightly, but trepidation echoed in its corners. *Was this individual a well-wisher? Or perhaps someone looking to manipulate Eli's story for their own ends?* The pulsing questions sparked an electricity in the air. The weight of possibility sat heavily, knowing this moment could change everything she thought she knew about Eli, his past, and even her own burgeoning feelings for him.

Staring at the screen, Anya felt her heart racing. Each thump reverberated, a stark reminder of how intertwined their destinies seemed to grow, and yet the unease thrummed alongside it. *Who was this person?* The keyboard beckoned, but her hands felt paralyzed, suspended between the urge to learn more and the rawness of uncertainty.

She stared at the screen, heart pounding, captivated by a mixture of thrill and trepidation. This was a moment she hadn't anticipated, waiting to bloom before her. *Would answering the inquiry unfurl something beautiful or risk unraveling the intricate tapestry she had woven around Eli and Clara's love story?* The air thickened as she weighed her options, the shadows of doubt looming large.

* * *

HER HEART DANCED WITH EXCITEMENT, fingers twitching as thoughts raced through her mind like a torrent. She couldn't contain the exuberance swelling within her. It felt almost electric, like she'd just stepped into a new chapter of the universe, one where Eli's past and her present intertwined in a way she never thought possible.

"Eli!" she called out, her voice ringing through the hushed air like a bell, the fervor dancing on her tongue. "You need to see this!"

Anya leaned forward, practically leaning off the edge of the chair where she perched. The idea that she might have stumbled upon a vital link to Eli's life sent a flutter through her chest. This wasn't just a discovery about a novel—it was about Eli himself, about Clara, about the love that seemed frozen in time. The sensations coursing through her made the air feel thick with possibilities. She felt buoyant, almost bouncing in her seat as she waited for Eli to materialize.

Seconds ticked by, stretching into an eternity. Anxiety drummed in her ears, each tick amplifying her urgency. *What if this was the breakthrough she'd longed for? What if Clara was closer than she ever imagined?* Her heart raced as she envisioned the potential stories of love, loss, and hope hidden behind Eli's past, stories that could breathe life into both their narratives.

Finally, the air shifted, and the shadows in the corner of the room flickered. Eli emerged from the depths, his form solid and striking against the wall of sunlight. His tousled dark hair caught the light, giving him an almost ethereal glow. Yet as he stepped fully into the room, Anya caught the subtle tension etched across his features. An eyebrow raised, he regarded her—a mixture of reflection and skepticism glimmering in his piercing blue eyes.

"What is it?" he asked, crossing his arms over his chest, a habitual gesture that shielded him, even now.

Anya couldn't help but grin wider, unable to contain her enthusiasm. "I got a message on my blog. Someone claims to know Clara! They said this story belongs to their family!"

Eli's expression shifted slightly, intrigue creeping in but mixed with a hint of caution. "Are you sure, Anya?"

"Yes, I'm sure, why wouldn't I be?"

"It's easy to misinterpret things," Eli replied, skeptical. "Especially when emotions are involved."

The weight behind his words hit her like a gust of wind, an unanticipated chill in the warmth of her excitement. She recognized his hesitance. It was an unspoken burden carried over from a past he could barely accept.

"I know it sounds unbelievable, but think about it!" Anya pressed, determination underscoring her voice. "This could be our chance to really understand what you—what Clara—went through. It might lead us to closure for both of you."

Eli took a measured step closer, the shadows swirling around him as if breathing in the tension that hung uncomfortably between them. "Closure?" The word fell from his lips like an uninvited guest. He tilted his head slightly, his expression now a bittersweet mixture of yearning and fear. "Digging into the past isn't always the answer, Anya. It may bring up things that are better left buried."

She felt the weight of his past fill the room. Anya could sense the walls he built around himself, the barriers he'd constructed to protect himself from reliving memories that teetered on the edge of his conscious—painful yet precious. She also understood the heavy legacy he carried; it wasn't just about his love story; it was about losses that intertwined with his identity and hers.

"But you deserve this," Anya responded gently, her voice barely above a whisper as she moved to close the distance between them. "You deserve to know the truth."

His gaze locked onto hers, a thousand unspoken questions swirling in his depths, each one tethered to his reluctance. It was a storm of emotions flickering behind the blue of his eyes; uncertainty battled with curiosity, longing danced with fear. "And what if the truth isn't what I hope it to be?"

Anya swallowed hard, her heart echoing a soft chaos in her chest. She wanted to assure him that it would be fine, but the truth carried no guarantees. "Sometimes, the truth can be painful, Eli," she replied, each word carefully chosen. "But holding onto the past without understanding it…that might hurt even more."

Anya's breath caught as the silence stretched between them, thickening like fog. Eli's anxious energy clashed with her hopeful spirit, creating an atmosphere that felt real. She held her breath, wishing he would step closer, to choose connection over solitude.

He ran a hand through his hair, his frustration simmering just out of sight. "You don't know me, Anya. Not completely."

"I'm trying to," she countered, stepping closer still, words pouring from her heart. "I want to understand you. I want to understand Clara. This writing—our connection—it's real. Every part of it is real."

His gaze softened, the armor around his heart momentarily wavering as he launched into deeper thoughts. "But what if

Clara's truth intertwines with anguish I'm not ready to face? What if it changes everything?"

It was a powerful juxtaposition—Eli, the ghost of a man longing for the connection to be rekindled yet haunted by the pain of what had been lost. Anya felt an urge to wrap her arms around him, to let him know he wasn't alone in these fears, but she hesitated, sensing the fragile ground they stood upon.

Anya paused, her heart twisting with an uncomfortable thought she had diligently avoided. She had danced around the edges of the question like it was a fragile vase, fearing that if she touched it too forcibly, it would shatter into a thousand pieces. Yet, the more she and Eli delved into their emotions and the fabric of their connection, the more the urge to know loomed like a shadow in a sunlit room.

How did he die?

The question loomed large, pressing against the walls of her mind. She noted the restraint in Eli's expression, the way he seemed to tread carefully through his memories, constructing them like delicate glass sculptures that could break with a single breath. But without knowing the truth, how could she fully understand the weight of his regrets and emotions?

"Eli," she began, her voice steady despite the racing of her heart. "Can I ask you a question?"

"Of course," he replied, his tone cautious as he tilted his head, the flicker of light catching in his eyes.

Anya took a deep breath, wrestling with the heaviness settling in her chest. "How did you… die?"

The atmosphere thickened instantly, as though the air had turned to stone, and Eli's expression shifted, shadowed by memories he had clearly kept tightly wound. He hesitated, the silence stretching longer than Anya anticipated as he processed her simple yet profound question. His gaze dropped momentarily, pain shimmering beneath the surface when he looked back at her.

"It's not an easy story to tell," he murmured, and the weight of his vulnerability hung in the air.

"No story worth sharing is easy," Anya replied, her voice barely above a whisper, an unspoken wish for him to confide in her, to let her into that hidden part of his existence.

Eli shifted slightly, the light in the room morphing as if trying to escape the shadows that swirled close to him. "We were driving," he began, his voice low and tinged with melancholy. "Clara was in the passenger seat. We were talking about what we wanted. College, marriage… The future."

Anya felt her heart clench at his words, envisioning their youthful faces—faces filled with dreams and uncertainty, navigating the cusp of adulthood. It was all too real. He had been so much more than just a ghost hovering in the corners of her life; he had once been a person just like her, with the same fears, driving through dreams and decisions.

"I… I chose college," Eli continued, his tone wavering. "I thought I needed to focus on that before anything else. I wanted to be a writer, and everyone said it was a path that required sacrifice. I didn't think it would devastate her. I didn't think…" He clenched his jaw, his expression twisting slightly, as though remembering the moment brought forth a fresh wave of anguish. "I never got to tell her I was sorry."

Anya's heart ached for him, for both of them. She could almost feel the weight of regret, thick and palpable, swirling around the room like an unwelcome fog. It hurt to listen to him recount that pivotal moment, to imagine the crushing disappointment written across Clara's face as those dreams and plans crumbled in a single, heart-wrenching realization.

"I…I didn't mean for it to happen," Eli confessed, his eyes glistening with unshed emotion. "The crash… I lost control of the car. I didn't see the tree until it was too late."

The vivid image struck Anya—Eli, gripping the steering wheel, panic rising in his chest, the looming reality of his decision crashing down like thunder. She closed her eyes for a brief moment, feeling the swift and sudden impact of his confession. A mix of sorrow and rage bubbled within her—a sorrow for him as he remained bound to the past, and a rage directed at the universe for the cruel hand it had dealt him: a choice that had been too heavy, and yet, tragically, something none of them could escape.

"Eli," she whispered, feeling lost in the depths of his pain. She wanted to reach out, to close the distance between the worlds they inhabited, bridging the gap of regret with understanding. "You didn't intend for any of this. People make choices, sometimes ones we regret…"

"I know that," he said sharply, frustration sharpening his voice. His expression was raw, the anguish spilling forth as he turned away, frustration radiating from him. "But my choice cost her everything. I was supposed to protect her. I should have been there for her. But instead, I abandoned her at the worst moment."

Anya felt her own heart crack open, realizing just how torn Eli was between the affection he held for her—this curiosity for something real, something living—and the haunting legacy he could not escape. It was the truth of love—deep and binding yet layered with complexity and despair.

"You didn't abandon her," she said firmly, pushing against the dark void between them. "You were young and faced with impossible choices. Love is messy and complicated, Eli. It doesn't always follow a straight path."

"Messy, complicating choices," Eli echoed, quiet anger flickering in his eyes. "And now it's too late for me to make things right."

The haunting weight of loss encased them, and Anya felt the energy shift, heavy with absolution and remorse. "What if your story isn't finished? What if you could still make amends, in some way?"

Eli met her gaze, the tension taut between them shifting almost imperceptibly, a flicker of hope battling through the shadows he'd created around his heart. Anya felt the air change slightly around them, as if for the first time in years, Eli was considering the possibility that redemption could linger even in the depths of despair.

12
the journey to clara

Anya stepped closer, her excitement spilling into the air of the hidden room like the warmth of sunlight filtering through the dusty windowpanes. Her bright green eyes sparkled with an intensity that could illuminate even the darkest corners of Dvor House.

"Eli, I just know," she insisted, her voice bubbling with conviction. "It's like a thread weaving through time, pulling me closer to your love." Each word resonated with a rhythm as if echoing the stories trapped within the very walls that witnessed Eli's heartache.

Eli looked at her, uncertainty flickering in his piercing blue eyes. He studied her earnest expression, searching for signs of doubt but finding none. Anya leaned forward, her heart thrumming in her chest. She couldn't shake the feeling that she had forged a genuine link with Clara, their energies intertwining like ivy climbing the side of the mansion.

"Clara's spirit has been calling to me," Anya continued, her voice dipping into a more intimate tone, urging Eli to understand the depth of her intuition. "I feel it every time I read those letters, every time I touch this notebook. If we reach out, if I connect with this person, we might uncover something beautiful—something that was lost." Her heart raced as she spoke, each word pulling Eli closer to her, intertwining their intentions.

Eli shifted his weight, a storm of conflicting emotions reflected in his gaze. Hope glimmered faintly against the tumult of doubt that brewed in his chest. "And what if we don't?" he asked quietly, his voice a mere whisper against the dusty glow of the sun filtering through the room.

Anya felt the weight of his question landing heavily in the air. She could sense a mixture of wariness and longing in him. Although he was a spirit tied to his past, she recognized the remnants of the young man who once had dreams, who had loved and lost that love far too soon.

"I believe reaching out is worth the risk," Anya countered softly, as if daring him not to believe in the potential for healing and understanding. "What we discover could bring Clara peace, maybe do the same for you. Don't you want to know?"

Eli closed his eyes for a moment, his expression pained. Memories surged within him, bubbling to the surface like old photographs. He felt the sunlight caressing his skin not as a ghostly touch but with a warmth reminiscent of summers spent with Clara. The laughter shared. The secrets whispered under starry skies. Each reminiscence twisted with an undercurrent of guilt, pulling at him with invisible strings.

"I do want to know," he finally admitted, his voice laced with emotion. "But what if I'm only keeping you tied to this world to feed my desire for unfinished business?"

Anya reached out, placing her hand on his arm, feeling the coldness of his presence clash with the warmth radiating from her own body. The fabric of the universe suddenly felt thin, the boundaries of the living and the dead fluttering like pages in the wind. "No," she assured him, her voice steady but gentle. "You're not keeping me here. I want to help because I care, Eli. About you, your story, and about Clara. It's so much bigger than just me. We can bring light into the shadows of your past together."

Eli's heart swelled at her words, but a deep-rooted fear pulsed beneath his surface. "What if Clara's spirit doesn't even want to be found?" he questioned. "I'm trapped in this endless loop of regret, and I don't want to pull you into that turmoil, Anya."

Anya met his gaze, feeling the weight of his fears. The swirl of emotions around them created a tension charged with possibility yet fraught with apprehension. "Eli, you've shared your fears with me, and I'm not afraid of yours," she assured him, her voice a soothing balm. "There's beauty in exploring these shadows. I can feel it! What if we can help Clara find the closure she needs? And you too?"

His heart tugged at her words. Hope seemed to shimmer just beyond the horizon of possibility, though skepticism remained an enticing shadow lurking in his thoughts. "Finding her means dredging up the past—painful memories, old wounds. Who knows what might emerge?"

The air around them felt heavy with unspoken promises. Anya took a deep breath, feeling the gravity of their conversation wrap around them like a thick fog. She saw glimpses of vulnerability in Eli's eyes, glimpses hinting at the battles he fought long before he had become a ghost.

"Eli," she breathed, her voice dipping to a conspiratorial whisper, "What if it hurts but also heals? We can't ignore that possibility. Isn't that worth finding out?"

He pondered her words, feeling a flicker of hope radiating from her. Maybes turned into what-ifs in his mind. For the first time in a long while, he found himself at a precipice—poised to leap into an unknown realm he had feared drowned in sorrow. Anya, vibrant and alive, reached toward him, radiating warmth as she spoke in a soft tone that melted away the echoes of regret.

"I think this could be a fresh start—not just a search for Clara but a chance for us," she said, an earnest light shining in her eyes. "You showed me how to write again, how to embrace my passion. Let's discover together who Clara was and what she means to you. The past shaped us, but it doesn't define us."

The sincerity in her gaze wove threads between them. Eli bowed his head, contemplating her words, and he felt a deep yearning beginning to awaken inside him, igniting curls of hope.

"I won't push you toward Clara if you don't want to go," Anya murmured, pulling back just slightly to gauge Eli's reaction. "But I believe uncovering who she is could free you from the shackles of grief. I want to help you heal."

He looked up, caught in a tender gaze that throttled the fears that had sat in his chest like stones. He saw not just Anya standing before him but an opportunity to loosen the grip of regret that had clung to him like a fog for too long. She was right, and the idea of allying their strength to uncover the love story hidden in the echoes of time felt almost magical.

After a few moments of silence shared between them, Eli finally nodded, and with that small gesture, belief seeped into the cracks that doubt had laid bare. "Alright. Let's find Clara. But promise me, Anya—when we do, we'll be gentle with whatever comes."

"Of course," Anya breathed, relief flooding her. The shadows flickered with a newfound path ahead, illuminated by the spark of friendship forged in the fires of uncertainty.

With determination set within them like an unyielding force, the pair braced themselves for what lay ahead in their journey, ready to uncover the forgotten pieces of a love story waiting to be told.

* * *

ANYA STEPPED CLOSER TO ELI, feeling the pull of their shared energy in the dim light of the hidden room. This space, once filled with dusty memories, was now a sanctuary of their connection—a bridge between two worlds. She sensed Eli's reluctance, the tightness in his jaw and the way his midnight-blue eyes flickered with uncertainty. An idea sparked within her, a way to break through the barrier that seemed to hold him back.

"What if there's something I could share with Clara that only you would know?" Anya ventured, her voice steady yet imbued with warmth. "A secret, a memory, something that could prove I truly understand her love?"

Eli's gaze faltered, turning inward as his mind began to swirl with possibilities. He inhaled sharply, caught off guard by Anya's suggestion. The implications dangled in the air, enticing yet daunting, as he wrestled with what to reveal. Anya observed the subtle shifts in his expression, noting the way he seemed to retreat slightly, as though unsure if this venture into vulnerability was a risk worth taking.

"Think about it, Eli." Anya's tone was tender, coaxing. "What's something special between you two? A shared moment, a phrase, anything that could resonate with her?"

Silence enveloped them, wrapping around Eli like a warm blanket, dense yet comforting. He pressed his lips together and turned his gaze to the floor, lost in thought. Memories cascaded around him—fragments of laughter, whispers under the stars, the sound of Clara's voice lilted by joy. They flowed like water, but hesitation stilled the waves, preventing him from diving deep.

Eli's posture softened as if Anya's words unlocked something dormant within him. He let the memories wash over him without resistance this time. In a small, hidden glade deep in the woods, he saw Clara cradling a delicate wildflower, that moment alive in his mind. She had bent close, her laughter shimmering in the moonlit air, softly teasing him about his serious demeanor. "Life is as fleeting as these blossoms, Eli," she said, her fingers brushing against the petals with reverence. "You don't want to miss a moment."

That memory struck him; it was that moment that crystallized the depth of their connection, an encounter where they had shared secrets under the jade canopy of trees. But, sharing it with Anya? Could he risk exposing that part of himself, which still felt like it belonged to another era?

"I…" He faltered, breath catching in his throat. "There was a place. A clearing in the woods, near the river…" He paused, searching for the right words, and Anya's bright, pensive gaze encouraged more. "Clara and I used to go there. It felt like our own world."

As Eli spoke, the atmosphere shifted; a delicate energy filled the air, a sense of ancient nostalgia weaving through the memories.

Anya leaned in, captivated, as he recounted the essence of that secret world. "We'd talk for hours, share everything." A nostalgia tinged with regret colored his voice. "One night, she picked a wildflower and said she'd keep it pressed between the pages of her favorite book. She talked about the power of words, how they could transcend time, much like stories."

Eli's eyes twinkled for a moment, yet the warmth was swift to dissipate, replaced by apprehension. "I don't know if it would mean anything to her now," he confessed, the weight of doubt pulling his gaze away. "What if it's too late?"

"No," Anya interjected, her voice firm yet gentle. "This could be exactly what she needs—a reminder that connection exists beyond the grave. Please, Eli, share it. She deserves to know."

Eli remained still, caught between his wish to protect Clara's spirit and the undeniable understanding Anya offered. He relished the thought that he could still reach beyond, but the fear of his own emotions left him hesitant. He had spent so long drifting in shadows, mourning the lost potential of his life, that the desire to engage with a living heart stirred conflicting impulses within him.

"What else?" Anya asked, her excitement bubbling over, encouraging him, tempting him to delve deeper into his memories.

Eli pinched the bridge of his nose as he tried to gather his thoughts. "There was this shared secret, a phrase we'd whisper to each other whenever we wanted to feel brave. *'Hearts don't forget.'* It was our reminder… that even if life turned chaotic, our love would endure."

Anya's eyes sparkled, and a smile broke through her uncertainty. "That's beautiful," she murmured, captivated by the idea of their connection transcending time. A bolt of inspiration surged through her, urging her to capture this emotion on paper. "Then let's bring it to Clara. If you share this with me, I can find a way to reach her. It could mean everything to her."

Eli blinked at her with unguarded sincerity, a crack in the weight of self-doubt. This girl, influenced by an uncanny intuition, beckoned him toward reconciliation. Clarity emerged from the remnants of his fear; maybe sharing his love for Clara would not shatter their memory but instead embolden it.

"Okay, Anya." His voice emerged barely above a whisper, but it was filled with resolve. "I'll share all of it—the stories, the moments. I'll help you reach her."

13
the response

*A*nya perched at the edge of her chair, every muscle in her body tense with anticipation. The soft glow of her laptop screen illuminated her face as she stared at the notification on her phone, a small rectangular box that held the promise of a connection that felt unreal. Her heart raced, thumping loudly against her ribcage as she clicked on the comment. It felt almost ritualistic—a merging of her world with the unseen.

With trembling fingers, she opened the message from Clara, her breath hitching in her throat.

"I can't believe you found my letters. How do you know Eli's story?"

The words flowed across the screen, cryptic and raw, wrapped tightly in disbelief and curiosity. Anya could almost envision Clara's expression, caught in a mix of pain and hope, a ghost grappling with shadows of her past. The weight of Clara's skepticism pressed against Anya: how could she possibly explain her connection to Eli? The swirling emotions within her granted her no easy answers.

What do I even say? Anya wondered as doubt coiled around her thoughts. Wasn't it ridiculous to believe that Clara—a woman from a bygone era—would be open to speaking with her? Still, beneath the question lay a burning determination, a flicker of defiance urging her to push beyond the veil of uncertainty. The connection she had with Eli felt tangible, stretching beyond the limits of time and existence.

She took a deep breath, her thoughts racing. Clara's skepticism struck a chord, sending a wave of nerves rustling through her. Suddenly, the enormity of the situation filled her chest with an unfamiliar weight. How could she convey the intensity of what she had felt while reading those letters? Her hand hovered over the keyboard, and Anya's mind filled with fragments of ideas, jumbled but alive.

"Do I really want this?" she whispered to herself, a moment of hesitation mingling with her yearning for connection. But she thought of Eli—his spirit, so vibrant yet filled with regret—and felt the gentle nudge of resolve guide her.

Anya closed her eyes briefly and drew in a stabilizing breath, gathering fragments of her thoughts like scattered leaves in a gust of wind. She opened her eyes, determined to compose a message that reflected both her sincerity and her respect for Clara—a woman whose love had transcended time.

After a few moments of quiet focus, she began to type, carefully selecting her words.

"Dear Clara,"

she started, her fingers dancing over the keys.

> "I hope this message finds you well, though I understand that may be a complex sentiment."

Careful now, Anya thought. She continued, weaving honesty into her words.

> "My name is Anya, and I've been discovering the remnants of your love story with Eli. Words can't quite capture how deeply they've affected me. I have a connection to Eli through his unfinished novel and a collection of letters filled with your shared emotions. I am a medium, and I've been granted the ability to see spirits, which is how I came to know about you both."

Each keystroke felt like peeling back layers of time, revealing the golden threads of love that had once bound Eli and Clara. Despite the profundity of her message, there was humility in Anya's words, echoing her reverence for their story.

> "I respect what you've shared,"

she typed, her heart hammering against her chest.

> "And I'm reaching out with the hope that you would consider sharing something more—if there's anything you wish Eli to know. A word, a feeling, a memory—anything that might help bridge the gap from the past to present."

Pausing, Anya looked at her screen, feeling the weight of her request settling like a whisper against the air. The tapping of her fingers had slowed, but determination ignited within her. She desperately wanted Clara to understand that she viewed their love story not as mere words in a book but as a living testament that mattered now more than ever.

With a soft exhale, she hit send, relief flooding over her as she leaned back in her chair. For a brief moment, she reveled in the feeling of connecting two worlds—the warmth of Eli's presence and the unyielding longing woven throughout Clara's reply.

And yet, an undercurrent of anxiety raced through her veins as the reality of her action settled into her bones. What if Clara dismissed her overtures? What if she was unwelcome, a trespasser in a story thick with heartache and memory?

Her mind spun with the possibilities, dancing between hope and dread. With each tick of the clock in the dimming light of Dvor House, she felt the silence grow heavier, amplifying the chaos in her heart. Every sound—the creak of the old wooden floors, the rustle of the curtains billowing gently in the breeze—felt amplified in the stillness, puncturing through her mounting anticipation.

The minutes dragged on, each tick of the clock sounding louder than the last, until the silence became almost unbearable. She glanced from her laptop to her phone intermittently, each beat of her heart punctuating her impatience.

Anya replayed the thought of Clara's message again and again, shivers filling the quiet space around her as her mind wandered. She could sense the weight of Clara's anguish, could almost share in it.

Time stretched endlessly until finally, her phone chimed, slicing through the tension like a knife through silk. She felt her breath catch as she furiously snatched it from the table, eyes wide as she looked down at a new notification.

Clara had responded.

Glimpses of excitement and trepidation danced within her as she opened the message. Her heart raced once more, a rollercoaster of emotions surging through her as she read the familiar name: "Clara."

The message, however, was more than that—it sparkled with an ethereal blend of longing, curiosity, and perhaps, a touch of hope. Anya bit her lip, excitement surging within her, ready to plunge deeper into the realms of love intertwined between those too long apart.

But uncertainty also tempered her eagerness. She thought of Eli and the bond they forged. What awaited her might very well alter the tapestry of their stories forever, echoing with the unresolved heartache of years gone by.

* * *

ANYA HELD her breath as she approached the little coffeehouse nestled on a corner just a block from her high school. It was quaint, its weathered brick façade softened by trails of climbing ivy. The sign hanging above the doorway swung gently in the breeze, a cheerful contrast to the tension coiling within her. Clara had agreed to meet her here, and Anya's heart raced at the thought of finally connecting with the spirit from Eli's past.

Inside, sunlight streamed through the windows, creating warm pools of light on the wooden tables. The rich aroma of freshly brewed coffee mingled with the sweet scent of pastries, creating a cozy atmosphere. Anya scanned the room, spotting a woman sitting at a corner table. Clara was *real*, a living human being. Her once vibrant youth written by Eli faded into wrinkles and a serene, aged elegance. A silver bun nestled loosely at the back of her head, and her eyes—sharp and blue—held traces of stories untold.

Taking a deep breath, Anya approached Clara's table, her excitement tempered by uncertainty.

"Clara?" Anya said softly.

The woman looked up, a hint of curiosity intermingling with skepticism in her gaze. "Yes. You must be Anya." Her voice was steady but laced with an undercurrent of disbelief.

Anya slid into the chair opposite her, feeling the weight of those sharp blue eyes. "Thank you for meeting me," she began, her heart thudding in rhythm with the distant sound of a train rolling past.

"Let's get one thing straight." Clara's voice was calm but firm. "I want to know how you know so much about my past with Eli."

Anya felt a knot tighten in her stomach. Clara's bluntness sparked a tension that felt almost tangible.

Reading her facial features, Clara grinned, "I'm old," she snickered, "us seniors don't have time to have no more filters."

"I understand," Anya laughed, channeling calmness into her tone. "Dvor House, the mansion Eli spent his life in. When I inherited the house, I found love letters he wrote to you."

Clara's expression shifted, skepticism renewed, her brows knitting together. "Letters? And you're some kind of… medium?"

"Yes." Anya's voice trembled just a bit as she continued, determined to stand her ground. "I inherited more than just the house. I inherited the ability to see and communicate with spirits. Eli's presence has been with me since day one—his memories and emotions are intertwined with the house, and writing has connected us. I felt compelled to learn more about him, about you."

"How can I trust you?" Clara's voice held a steely resolve that cut through the air. "You could just be some trickster who thinks it's fun to toy with the past."

Pain shot through Anya. She leaned forward, infusing her words with sincerity and warmth. "I don't want to trick you. I want to understand." She reached for the stack of love letters resting in her bag, her fingers brushing against the delicate pages. "Eli loved you, Clara. So deeply. He never stopped thinking about you. I read the letters, and they paint a picture of a passionate connection, filled with warmth and longing. I'm here to honor that."

Clara blinked, caught off guard by the emotion that seeped into Anya's tone. The room fell silent as her defenses flickered, and Anya could almost feel the tension thawing between them. Perhaps Clara was beginning to see the truth in her eyes.

"I was young," Clara said slowly, her voice softening as if the weight of years pressed down on her. "I was just sixteen when we loved like that. And now…" Her voice trailed off, lost in memories that seemed to drift like smoke.

"What was it like?" Anya asked, her heart swelling with curiosity. "What do you remember?"

Clara's blue eyes glimmered as she reminisced. "Eli was everything to me." A wistful smile grazed her lips before the gravity of her expression returned. "We laughed so much, shared dreams, little promises just like kids do. But then…" The thought seemed to crumble her. "The crash took him from me."

Heavy silence lingered in the air between them as Anya felt her own heartache for the loss they had both felt.

"Did you ever get to say goodbye?" she whispered.

Clara closed her eyes for a moment, as if allowing herself to dwell in a memory. "No. Not the way I wanted to. It was all so sudden." Tears gathered in her eyes, but she blinked them away, her voice steadier than before. "I was in the hospital when I learned he died, it left me with regrets—things I wish I'd done, words I wish I'd said."

Anya shifted forward, leaning in, her heart racing as she took the plunge. "Do you have anything you'd like to say to Eli now?" The words felt fragile as they left her lips, yet the air thickened with an electric charge, a connection forming between the past and present.

Clara hesitated, her lips pressing together before she replied. "I've thought about it so many times. But after all these years, I don't know if it still means anything." Uncertainty danced in her eyes.

"Maybe it does," Anya urged softly, her own heart beating rapidly. "Sometimes the heart doesn't let go, even when life moves on. What if there's something you need him to know?"

The atmosphere shifted, tension and vulnerability intertwining as Clara's defenses began to crack further. "I don't even know how he could hear me," Clara said quietly, her voice almost a whisper now.

Anya felt the weight of Clara's words, clinging to her own hope. "He senses you, Clara. I see the emotions between you. The unfinished promise woven into the fabric of time. Whatever you fear sharing doesn't matter—it's human to love and grieve."

Silence settled between them, wrapping them in a shroud of

shared emotion. Clara gazed down at her hands, trembling slightly, as the shadows of her past crept into the light.

14
clara's heartfelt confession

Anya sat at the small round table tucked in the corner of the coffeehouse, the warm aroma of freshly brewed beans enveloping her senses. The hustle and bustle of patrons faded into a distant hum as she focused on Clara, who flickered like a candle in the dim light. The ghostly figure appeared fragile, the shape of her being draped in nostalgia.

"Take your time," Anya encouraged softly. "You're ready to share."

Clara's gaze drifted down to the surface of the table, fingers tracing the grain of the wood as if the texture could somehow ground her in this moment. Anya could feel the tension, the weight of decades pulling at Clara, but also something flickering —a spark of hope that had been buried beneath layers of sorrow.

"I never thought..." Clara began, her voice barely above a whisper. "After all this time, I'd have a chance to speak to him again."

Taking a breath, she hesitated, the words clinging to her throat. The weight of memories flooded the air between them, and Anya leaned closer, her heart swelling with empathy. She reached for Clara's hand—the gesture was comforting, even if it felt like grasping at mist.

"Please, Clara. Let him hear you. He needs this just as much as you do. You both deserve closure," Anya urged gently, inviting the sadness sitting in the room to shift. "You can bridge that distance that time has created."

Clara nodded slightly, tears forming in her translucent eyes. "It's just… what if he doesn't forgive me?" The tremor in her voice cut through Anya, a poignant reminder of the hurt lingering in their shared history.

"Love isn't about blame," Anya replied, her voice comforting yet firm. "It's about understanding, connection. It's about what you shared together; your love can survive the gaps."

As Clara swallowed down her emotion, the atmosphere around them became electric, as if the universe itself was waiting with bated breath. Anya felt a flicker of something magical—a connection forged in love, pain, and the healing power of truth. The table felt like a bridge between Clara and Eli, their pasts intertwining as if time no longer mattered.

Clara took a deep, shuddering breath as her gaze locked onto Anya's. "Hearts don't forget," she whispered, the words heavy with meaning. "I never forgot him, not for a moment. Even when I had to keep living."

The words dripped with centuries of loneliness, the ache of a million unsaid things, and Anya felt her own heart constrict in response. "Then let him know that," she responded, her own voice trembling with the weight of this timeless moment. "Let him know that your heart has always been his."

Clara's breath caught, and for a heartbeat, the air shimmered with possibility. With a quivering voice that seemed to resonate from the very essence of her being, Clara began her revelation. "Eli, I… I am so sorry. I wanted to protect you, protect what we had. I wanted to fight for us." Her fingers, though ghostly, appeared to grip the table with fierce intensity. "But I failed you, and I never stopped loving you."

The essence of her love poured out, an ethereal current that danced in an invisible space between Anya and Clara. The very air felt charged with emotion.

"The pain of losing you has lingered in my heart," Clara continued, her voice strengthening with each word. "I recognize now that I can't keep holding on to the past without it consuming me. I've missed you every day, and not a moment has passed without a thought of what we could have shared, what we could have fought for together."

Anya watched Clara, spellbound by the depth of the confession—a whirlwind of raw, unfiltered emotion. Each word was an echo of her own longings and fears as she navigated her connections with both Eli and Jake. "This is beautiful, Clara," she breathed, intoxicated by the gravity of their exchange.

"And I don't want my unfinished story to be one marred by regret," Clara added, her voice clear yet soft, the sincerity wrapping around Anya like a warm embrace. "Eli, hearts don't forget. They carry pieces of one another. They endure, whether it be through distance or death. And I want you to know… I've always loved you."

The finality of Clara's words sent a shiver through Anya. The truth, tender and poignant, lingered in the air like a promise renewed. She could feel a stirring within herself, a belief that their connection sparked something profound, something transcending the boundaries of time.

With every heartbeat, Anya sensed the fragile strings tying together love and memory, ghost and girl, past and present. Clara's melancholy ebbed into the ether, content in the vulnerability of having shared her heart. "Now I feel like I can finally let go," Clara whispered.

Anya nodded, feeling tears building in her own eyes. "You've given him a gift, Clara. A chance to understand. A chance to heal."

Clara's face brightened for a moment as she regarded Anya with gratitude. "Thank you for helping me find the courage to speak. You've pulled me from shadows I thought I'd never escape."

Anya felt the warmth of Clara's words wash over her, and she couldn't help but smile. "Love is powerful. It binds us in ways we can't always see."

The two women shared a moment of silence, the depth of their exchange threading an unbreakable bond—a connection that transcended the ordinary. Clara's delicate form shimmered slightly, a glow embodying the essence of her truth.

"I hope Eli knows how much I've loved him," Clara murmured softly, gazing into the distance, as if envisioning Eli's face.

Anya shifted, feeling the air settle into a tranquil silence—one filled with possibility. "He will, and with it, you both can find peace."

As Anya absorbed the enormity of what they had exchanged, the last strands of tension began to dissolve—love transcended time, rekindling hope for both Clara and Eli. The echo of Clara's confession hung in the air, leaving Anya breathless, urging her to keep the conversation going and share this momentous shift with the boy trapped in the mansion's memories.

But she knew it required the strength to embrace everything that came with it, for both of them. There was a shimmer of something alive—an optimism that sparked from Clara's heartfelt confession, an invitation to continue the legacy of love that Clara and Eli had forged so long ago.

15

two weeks later

Anya stood outside Dvor House, her heart fluttering with a mix of excitement and nervousness. Weeks had passed since she last walked through its weathered entrance, since she had plunged into the depths of Clara's story, their bittersweet love echoing in her thoughts. The time apart felt like a wilderness, each day stretching longer as anticipation gnawed at her insides. She had almost convinced herself it might be easier to wait longer, to allow the messages from Clara to settle into something tangible, but urgency propelled her forward.

As she approached the grand entrance, she paused briefly, absorbing the familiar sight of ivy-clad stone and the tall, arched windows that had both enchanted and intimidated her. It struck her how radically her life had transformed since that first day—the lonely girl on the cusp of self-discovery had become a writer, an artist carving out her own path. The connection she forged with Eli felt sacred. It was a relationship that had bloomed beneath the shadows of the mansion, intertwining with the stories of the past.

With a deep breath, Anya grasped the heavy door handle, its weight symbolic of the burden of secrets waiting within. The door creaked open, and as she stepped inside, the familiar scents of dust and old wood wrapped around her like an embrace. The atmosphere felt charged with a hopeful expectation, as if the very walls anticipated her arrival and Eli's presence.

She moved through the grand foyer, her footsteps echoing against the tiled floor, the sound reverberating as though the house itself greeted her return. "Eli, it's me, Anya! I'm back—I need to talk to you!" Her voice trembled slightly as it echoed into the air, tinged with longing. She half-expected the soft flicker of his presence to envelop her, the warmth of his spirit wrapping around her like a nostalgic blanket.

Anya's heart raced, rising and falling with every moment of silence. Her gaze darted around the expansive room, searching for any sign of him—anything to suggest that she hadn't come here in vain. Yet, the silence hung heavily, thick with the absence of the ghost she had come to know. Her pulse quickened as worry settled over her like a fog, stirring in her chest, while the echoes of her voice faded into nothingness.

She touched her fingers gently to the wall, feeling the rough texture beneath her soft skin, trying to embrace the history that coursed through the very fabric of the mansion. "Eli?" She murmured to herself, the chill of isolation creeping in. "Where are you?" The sense of emptiness weighed heavily; the echoes of joy they shared felt distant and out of reach.

Anya swallowed her fears, steeling herself with determination. If Eli wasn't here, that didn't mean he wouldn't come. Resolute, she made her way through the mansion, heart set on finding the hidden room that had become their sanctuary—a place where words, ghostly whispers, and emotions flowed freely. Each step resonated with purpose as she traced the path that led to the narrow staircase hidden behind the tattered curtain.

Reaching the door, she pushed it open with a familiar flourish, entering the sun-drenched sanctuary filled with endless possibilities. The remnants of love letters lay scattered across the table, a sea of ink and emotion begging to be understood. The unfinished novel rested in the corner, its pages a testament to Eli's passion for storytelling. Anya stepped into the room's embrace, feeling the presence of history swirl around her.

"Eli," she whispered, centering herself once again. "Please, I need you here with me. I have something important to share." The quiet room absorbed her words, leaving behind a tinge of desperation that tingled in the air. She looked around, willing him to materialize, but again, emptiness echoed back at her.

Anxiety began to creep into her bones, dulling her excitement. Anya shut her eyes momentarily, taking a deep breath, and focusing on the world within. Cast into the depths of the silence —a world where she felt so alone without his presence—she determined not to let doubt cloud her heart. "Eli, I know you're here, somewhere. You're not gone, not yet."

Finding a comfortable spot on the worn, sunlit floor, she settled cross-legged, letting air fill her lungs in slow, deliberate inhales and gentle exhales. It was a meditation she had employed before, a tethering of energies that fused her heart and mind into a space for Eli's spirit to draw near. Somewhere in this vastness, she hoped to spark the connection they had forged.

As she steadied her breath, Anya visualized the warmth of Eli's presence, calling it forth through their shared memories—the laughter, the inspirations, and the sorrow binding them. Time and again, she had felt the brush of his energy against her skin as he whispered stories from a past she was eager to unearth. The room began to shimmer, a subtle pulse rippling through the air, carrying with it a sense of vitality.

Anya clung to the hope that this moment would be different, that her intentions would be enough to summon him forth. Each breath propelled her deeper into that vision, a visualization of love and longing wrapped in Clara's messages. Tucking those sentiments into her visualization, the power of their emotions began to bloom like flowers unfurling their petals for sunlight.

The atmosphere shimmered beneath her closed eyelids, and for the briefest moment, Anya could almost feel it—the warmth of Eli's spirit drawing closer, his essence overlapping with her own. A tension hung in the air, alive and electric, as she poured her heart into the silence around her.

The door suddenly creaked behind her, and a gentle breeze stirred the air, filling her lungs with an otherworldly presence. Anya's heart raced, hope igniting once more as she remained in her meditative state, feeling the movements and nuances of something ethereal brushing through the hidden room. She opened her eyes, penetrating the charged atmosphere with an eager gaze, hoping to glimpse the figure she longed for.

"Eli?" Anya called, her voice echoing softly, filled with longing and anticipation as she settled deeper into the moment, embracing the unknown that lay ahead.

*** * * ***

THE ATMOSPHERE THICKENED around Anya as she remained in the dimly lit hidden room, seeking connection with Eli. Meditative breaths settled her racing heart until the air turned frigid, an unmistakable sign that Eli was near. She opened her eyes, just in time to witness him materializing before her—a figure aglow with an otherworldly light that seemed to radiate warmth against the chill. Relief surged through her like a tidal wave.

"Eli!" she breathed, unable to mask the joy in her voice.

But before she could collect her thoughts, another presence coalesced beside him, and Anya gasped.

Clara…

She emerged, ethereal and radiant, with a beauty that transcended time. Anya's jaw dropped as she realized they were united, their hands entwined. The sight spilled over her heart like warm sunlight, both beautiful and deeply profound.

In that moment, everything aligned—the loves, the losses, the stories that wove through their lives. They stood together, Eli and Clara, a testament to love unbroken by the passage of time. It felt as if the world had narrowed down to just the three of them, each thread connecting them in a way Anya had never fully understood before.

Eli met her gaze, a soft smile breaking across his lips, filled with gratitude that challenged the boundaries of words. "Anya," he whispered, emotion coursing through his voice like a melody that brought tears to her eyes, "thank you for bringing Clara back to me."

She saw Clara's face light up as she sighed, pure affection reverberating in her words. "I longed for this moment, my Eli. Every moment apart was filled with love for you. I'm so sorry for the pain that lingered." Clara's voice carried the weight of centuries yet remained warm like a gentle breeze.

Anya's heart swelled as understanding settled in. The pieces of her journey, from feeling like an outsider to becoming part of something eternal, came together in harmonious clarity. She finally recognized the significance of her bond with Eli, not simply as a quest to help him find closure, but as part of a broader narrative about love, loss, and healing.

Eli turned to Clara then, their expressions filled with an intimacy that spoke of shared memories and heartache. Anya felt like an intruder at first, yet she quickly recognized her role—she had become the bridge connecting two beloved souls.

In that moment, clarity enveloped her like the softest of blankets. It was as if the weight of their unfinished story was lifting, transforming the heaviness into something light. A genuine sense of joy emerged in her chest, wrapping around her thoughts like vines climbing toward the sun.

With the electric tension in the air dissipating, Anya watched as Eli and Clara drew closer together, lost in each other's gaze, as though the years apart had melted away in the warmth of their reunion.

Anya felt honored, witnessing this beautiful display of love, a validation of all their struggles and sacrifices. She kept silent, simply observing the connection born from years of yearning. This moment of profound healing felt sacred, a gift she never anticipated.

"Thank you, Anya," Eli murmured, his eyes shining with newfound light, as if he had just escaped from a deep slumber. "You have always been the bridge."

Their eyes locked onto hers, a familial warmth extending into the space between them, wrapping around her like an embrace. Anya felt tears prick at the corner of her eyes, overwhelmed with emotion.

"Remember," Eli added, his voice softer now, "hearts don't forget."

Clara mirrored his sentiment, her voice ethereal yet firm, "You have given us what we needed, Anya. You'll always hold a piece of our story."

And just like that, it happened. Eli's and Clara's forms began to shimmer, their outlines blurring like clouds dissolving under the dawn's light. The glow around them brightened and pulsed, resonating with the love that transcended their mortality. Anya stood breathless, a spectator to their magic, until, in a heartbeat, they became one with the brilliance surrounding them.

As the light gradually dimmed, she was left standing in the hidden room, filled with both the ache of bittersweet longing and the joy of knowing she had played a pivotal part in their reunion. A warmth flooded through her; it felt lighter now, the heaviness of their unfinished business at last lifted.

Anya's heart brimmed with peace, realizing that although she had facilitated this ethereal moment, her journey was far from over. The love shared between Eli and Clara coursed through her, energizing her words and fueling her own narrative as a writer.

Setting her sights back to the unfinished manuscript of Eli's novel, Anya picked up her pen with renewed determination, ready to forge her path and chronicle Eli's story, infusing the themes of love and healing into her own. This was her legacy now —an intertwining of voices across realms.

Just then, Anya heard a soft, unexpected knock at the front door. She paused mid-thought, her heart fluttering with intrigue.

Curiosity lured her away from her writing. She set down her pen, smoothing her hair back as she made her way towards the door. *Who could it be?* In her mind, echoes of excitement ebbed alongside the residual warmth from the moment she had just witnessed.

Swinging the door open, she was greeted by Jake, standing there with an easy smile that lit up his face. "Hey, Are you hungry?" He asked, energy radiating from him like the sun's rays breaking through clouds.

Anya felt an involuntary smile tug at her lips as he reached out and took her hand gently, leading her outside. The warmth from their touch melded seamlessly with the lingering magic from the hidden room, igniting a different sort of thrill in her heart. She was ready for whatever came next, balancing the remnants of Eli's story with her future, one step at a time.

THE END

journey to crystal lake - part one

escape the ordinary. find your spark.

Get swept away with Journey to Crystal Lake, a thrilling YA romance in two parts!

Maddie's annual camping trip takes a dramatic turn when a blizzard tears through the mountains, separating her from her family. Lost and alone, she finds herself in a deserted cabin... with Dex, the infuriatingly handsome boy from school who secretly holds her heart.

Will they find their way back together, or will the storm ignite a bitterness even fiercer than the blizzard?

Part One!

Young Adult Romance

by Lia Lucas

Ebook & Paperback

snowbound with the boy next door

PART TWO

adventure awaits...

Maddie's annual camping trip takes a dramatic turn when a blizzard tears through the mountains, separating her from her family. Seeking refuge in a deserted cabin, she encounters the last person she expects – Dex, the infuriatingly handsome boy from high school and the campsite next door.

Sparks fly in the face of danger...

Forced to rely on each other for survival, Maddie and Dex's contrasting personalities clash at first. But as the storm rages on, shared stories and flickering candlelight ignite an unexpected warmth between them.

Will their love weather the storm?

With dwindling supplies and no way to contact help, their newfound connection faces its ultimate test. Can their bond survive the harsh reality of their situation, or will it melt away like the snow?

Discover a captivating story of resilience, adventure, and unexpected love.

Part Two!

Young Adult Romance

by Lia Lucas

Ebook & Paperback

star-crossed rivals

opposites attract. or repel.

Avery's the golden child.

Noah's the rebel with a cause. They hate each other. But when forced to partner for the school's Shakespeare competition, their world collides.

Will sparks fly, or will their rivalry consume them?

Dive into a captivating tale of love, hate, and everything in between.

Opposites attract...or do they? Find out in this sizzling YA romance.

Ebook & Paperback

haunted hearts

a summer camp. a tragic past. a ghost with an unfulfilled longing.

Can you feel a chill?

Riley thought summer camp would be filled with friends, campfires, and maybe a little flirting. But when she arrives at the rumored haunted camp, she discovers a secret world beyond her wildest imagination. There, she encounters the ghost of a dashing young counselor, trapped between the living and the dead.

As their connection deepens, Riley must navigate the complexities of a forbidden love while unraveling the chilling mystery surrounding the ghost's tragic demise. Will their love story be a haunting memory or a chance for redemption?

Prepare to be captivated by a tale of love, loss, and the supernatural.

Young Adult Romance

Ebook & Paperback

about lia

Lia Lucas is an emerging author of Urban Fiction, Young Adult, and Contemporary Romance. She has a wide range of writing interests and is currently living an incognito digital lifestyle.

Ms. Lucas is part of the Ardent Artist Books family.

Lia has published several books.

youtube.com/theardentartist
amazon.com/stores/Ardent-Artist-Books/author/B08BX8F1DZ

also by lia

YOUNG ◆ ADULT

Journey To Crystal Lake - Part One

Snowbound with the Boy Next Door - Part Two

Star-Crossed Rivals

* * *

SERIES

The Haunted Hearts Series

Haunted Hearts - Book 1

Ink and Ashes - Book 2

Ghosts in the Attic - Book 3

* * *

18+ ◆ Adult

Curves

She Was Going Home

www.ingramcontent.com/pod-product-compliance
Lightning Source LLC
LaVergne TN
LVHW012021060526
838201LV00061B/4405